DOWN IN THE HOLE,

THE UNWIRED WORLD OF
H.B. OGDEN;

BEING BOTH A TRUE AND ACCURATE ACCOUNT OF THE LIFE, WORK AND STRUGGLES OF FORGOTTEN
JOURNALIST AND FICTION WRITER H.B. OGDEN, WITH EMPHASIS UPON HIS GREATEST WORK, THE FIVE-
VOLUME SERIAL NOVEL

THE WIRE,

GENEROUSLY EXCERPTED WITHIN;

TO WHICH IS ADDED A SELECTION OF INTERESTING

ILLUSTRATIONS AND
ANALYTICAL WRITINGS

COMPOSED RESPECTIVELY BY ORIGINAL "THE WIRE" ILLUSTRATOR "BUBZ" BAXTER BLACK
AND BY THE PRESENT VOLUME'S AUTHORS:

JOY DELYRIA

AND

SEAN MICHAEL ROBINSON

POWERHOUSE BOOKS
BROOKLYN, NY

PUBLISHERS OF MANY FINE VOLUMES OF
ETCHINGS, ENGRAVINGS, POETRY, &C, OF BOTH
HISTORICAL AND CONTEMPORARY VINTAGE.

2012

Foreword by Henry Flowers, Sterling Professor of Literature at Princeton University

_____

On the Canon, The Wire, and the Worthy

You hold in your hand a rare thing; excerpts from and competent critical analysis of a work of some literary merit that has somehow escaped the inevitably just and continually active process of literary Canonization. The Canon, which Kermode famously identified as "negat[ing] the distinction between knowledge and opinion," is the process by which writers and critics, and on occasion other readers with aesthetic acuity, enshrine the worthiest of literary works—those of deepest characterization and most potent aesthetic virility—so that they may be passed down to future persons of intelligence. It is, in short, survival of the strongest, most vigorous writing. A culling, a strengthening and buttressing of the great human Aesthetic Enterprise through the annihilation of the unworthy. If a work of literature has entered the Canon, it is nothing less than a survivor of a three thousand year cosmomeritological slaughter, a war that has left the life work of tens of thousands of literary mediocrities abandoned to the abattoir.

And yet, in the midst of our crumbling institutions of "higher learning," currently choked with bitter Scholars of Resentment that savage the Canon at every opportunity with the Ism of their choice, come two scholars of alleged intelligence and judgment seeking to enlarge the Canon on an aesthetic rather than a political basis. This text is their attempt. They do not seek to Engorge the Canon as their brothers in Isms do by entering the unworthy—rather, they say, in this, the rarest of cases, Aesthetic and Cultural justice was not done—the worthiest work, the fittest work, was not identified, and in fact has narrowly escaped destruction.

Is such a thing possible? Could a worthy work of strong Literary Originality have escaped enshrinement? Let us skip over the endlessly repeated story of The Wire's rediscovery and instead address this point. In my book The Excrutiating Agony of Influence *(Princeton University Press, 1983), I argued convincingly that Canonization is impossible without influence, that the process of selection is carried out by future generations of writers and critics who selectively feed or starve the works of the past by the Literary Fathers with which they torturedly grapple. In this Darwinian/Freudian model of Patranatural Selection no figure looms larger than the Stratford Man himself, who with his 38 plays taught us more than any human that ever lived, who in fact single-handedly created Mod-*

ern Cognition. A person completely free of the influence of Shakespeare would be more great ape than modern man, and thus all writers carry the burden of that heavy debt. And so it must be so, in a lesser way, with all works in the Canon. How can a work enter the canon without having extended its tendrils of influence into that fertile soil of brain, paper and ink?

It is beyond possibility that a literary force as intensely luminous and nakedly blinding as a Shakespeare or a Milton or a Dante could be obscured beneath the bushel basket of time. But what of the lesser of those mighty lights? What of a Voltaire or an E. Brontë or a Dickens? The last two are most germane to the discussion, as both were contemporaries of the author under scrutiny. How does The Wire, the six year literary labor of that almost-forgotten agitator H.B. Ogden, compare to the output of Dickens, with whom he apparently enjoyed a spirited if primarily imaginary rivalry? And perhaps more importantly, if we accept the aesthetic judgment of DeLyria and Robinson that Ogden was equal to or even greater than his more famous foe, how do we justify his long exclusion from the Canon? Is Ogden essentially to be treated as a contemporary writer, as his influence on writers of subsequent generations has so far been negligible? Will further judgment on this matter have to wait until future generations of aestheticians have had the time to digest this unearthed work?

These are questions for another generation of readers, a generation which may not ever exist if our intellectual Parade of Resentment continues its plunge into the gorge of Historical Injustice. As to the aesthetic issues, however, the considerations are many and varied. As DeLyria and Robinson defensively explain several times in their analysis, Ogden is unafflicted by the rabble-pleasing sentimentality that clings to so much of Dickens' output. This is in itself no great virtue, though, nor are his use of the great themes or his undoubtedly heartfelt if misguided social concerns, not if his writing itself is not of the utmost muscularity and strength, his prose as worthy of that great man whose words and characters continue to grace the bookshelves of learned and squalid alike. Is Ogden such a man? DeLyria and Robinson say yes. As for myself, I am no soothsayer, and I will resist the urge to speculate as to the future influence of Ogden's epic tragiofarcical polemic.

I will say, however, that it is within the realm of the possible that DeLyria and Robinson are right, that the literary light of The Wire and the reputation of its author will burn brighter for the next generation of aesthetic elites than it has for those of the generation to which it belonged. To my admittedly historically limited judgment, Ogden's prose is adequate to his task and occasionally exceptional, especially in the descriptions of those structures of society against whom he set himself. However much he railed against the sentimental tendencies of his imagined rival, Ogden seems afflicted with his own kind of groundling-thrilling populism, that of the Spectacle of Violence. Like Poe, another Canon aspirant of uncertain standing, Ogden's art is sometimes equal to the task of mitigating his baser instincts. For all of its violence and grotesque spectacle, in sophistication The Wire is still leagues beyond the limitless orgy of viscera and gyration that assaults simpletons every night through the white-light delivery mechanism of their television set. Of that truly modern horror the less written the better—stringing together even a single coherent paragraph regarding that avalanche of dissipation is well beyond my own not unconsiderable powers of patience. It is perhaps a task best left to the undereducated and over-employed: specifically, my Colleagues of Resentment, who will not stop until every Department of Literature has been destroyed, to be replaced by yet another temple to "Cultural Studies."

And to what supplicants do these "academic" temples address themselves? Departments dwindle; attendance shrinks. The attention span of each incoming class of students is ever more fragile and withered than that of the prior. And these High Priests of Cultural Studies insist that theirs is the way out, that despite all evidence arrayed against them, theirs is the true key to Intellectual Enlargement, a kind of New Populism.

But we, the last few faithful followers of the Aesthetic alone, know the truth, that analyzing movies or romance novels or, heaven forbid, a television show, is to place one's nose directly into the evacuating orifice of the ascendant culture. Perhaps this is an easier task for my colleagues, whose every organ of perception seem to have atrophied from disuse, but for a person with refined aesthetic judgment a soap opera or a cops-and-robbers television program is nothing but an artefact for future historians, no more revealing than a yellowed bottle of dish detergent or a fossilized piece of excrement.

We know, instead, that the only true populism can come through the works of the great and the worthy, and that there was never nor will there ever be a greater populist than that greatest of writers, and greatest of human beings, the Bard without whom we would all be diminished, whose aesthetic supremacy is confirmed by 400 years of universal appeal and acclaim. When voices come forth calling for the opening of the Canon, let us pause and consider Shakespeare, that greatest of lights and most generous of Creators, and greatest of levelers, who speaks to scholar and ignoramus alike. We do not know if time will treat Ogden differently on this, his second improbable go-round, whether he will gain a new ascendency or be covered again by the shroud of the unknown, but we do know that either way, it will be time, and not any individual, that will be his judge.

INTRODUCTION

You know your Homer; you know your Virgil. You know your Chaucer, your Dante, your Shakespeare. You're well acquainted with Dickens, Tolstoy, Balzac; time has seen fit to familiarize you with James, Hawthorne, with Nabokov—who made room for himself with elbows and nary an, "Excuse me, please." But do you know Horatio Bucklesby Ogden?

You won't find him on your shelf next to your Cervantes or your Goethe; you won't find him in the essays of illustrious scholars. You won't find him taught in classrooms, or in the Penguin series of classics. You might, just possibly, find him in a dusty shelf of a library, beside a Meredith or Swinburne or someone else no one reads any more, but you won't find him in circles that style themselves literary. Nor will your find him in numerous spin-offs: films, television series, graphic novels, video games or cash-in mash-ups, where all the old classics go to die and be reborn as ads on toilet stalls.

Canon, you see, has entirely neglected to extend an invitation to Horatio Bucklesby Ogden, and that's how you've escaped an introduction. In another 150 years, everyone will assume that *The Wire*, that five volume Victorian masterpiece penned by Ogden, was just another bit of serial dreck published in a penny dreadful—never awarded any accolades by those who mattered, and thus forgotten by subsequent generations. We'll never have the sequel penned by some clever, aspiring grad student; we'll never have the action figure; we never got the film—though once, one man tried.

To find out how it came to this, we must go back in time, to the days of *The Wire*'s serialization in the mid-nineteenth century. A scattered few praised the work; some circles of society seemed to enjoy it very much. Perhaps it was H.B. Ogden himself who turned off the rest of the population, but so little is known of the man himself, it's difficult to say. When a man's work falls into obscurity, so too does his life; the two are intimately connected, as though the history of a man might work as a translation for his art. This isn't true: all men die; but some art lives on and on.

Charles Dickens was a great man and well-loved by many; he was known for his skills as an orator and for his theatricality. Emily Brontë was not a great woman, but we remember her for her family, the romance of her childhood, the gothic setting of her upbringing, the untimeliness of her death. H.B. Ogden is known for nothing save a title beside his name in a card catalogue; he is not Dostoevsky, the epileptic excused at the last minute from hanging, not Byron, a club foot with a love life unparalleled. He is not Homer, nor Shakespeare, those great bards who may have been many men, in fact, who may have never existed at all.

H.B. Ogden was just a man, struggling to make sense of a world full of cities that were changing, a time of building-up that went hand in hand with the makings of decay. We seek to discover that man: first, in what little details we could gather of his life, together with that of his illustrator, Baxter Black. Their lives are not an illustration: Black brings life to the work of Ogden in a way that mere collections of facts never can. In illuminating the creator of *The Wire*, we only wish to show that he was a man of his times.

Then again, perhaps it wasn't Ogden at all who made the work apparently inaccessible; the idea that it was Black has occurred to us as well. What little detail we have unearthed suggests Black was a soft-spoken man, but his illustration was not similarly gentle. Perhaps the violence of his art, or the characters on which he chose to so lovingly dwell, were in some way out of step with the time period Ogden so illuminates. It could be, we suppose, that Victorian audiences weren't ready to see the subject matter that *The Wire* portrayed in so much thorough, unrelenting detail.

We have attempted to address this subject matter, pulling apart those intricate threads in order to find the meaning of *The Wire*. It has been suggested that the complexity of the work itself made it unpalatable to the general public, and yet the final determinants of what must be considered "canon" remain unclear.

If the public has neglected *The Wire*, then we must also place the blame at the feet of scholars. *The Wire* has received some attention, but it deserves a place among the greats. It wouldn't be out of place on a shelf with Swift or Flaubert; it wouldn't even be out of place on a more modern book shelf, beside Gabriel Marquez or Pynchon. The best art is for all times, and *The Wire* is among the best.

The Wire is a novel, though it has not withstood the test of time. History has shot it down, declared it unworthy. But we declare, as those few enlightened souls have done before us: it is an injustice. This work deserves to be considered just as any Proust or any Plutarch, just as any Defoe or Dickens.

Where possible, text quoted from The Wire *is taken from the 1853 edition. The 1935 edition has only been used in those infrequent circumstances in which the first edition was too damaged to accurately transcribe.*

All illustrations are from the 1853 edition.

From BOOK I
Excerpt CHAPTER IV. "Old Cases."
(June 23, 1846)

[. . .] the landlord having let them in the door; thereupon they entered a bleak little place, lit only by a pale, sickly beam of sunlight streaming through the window. The meagre accommodation did nothing to placate the dissatisfaction of Mr McNulty, who—having voiced this complaint to Mr Moreland before having entered the crime scene—despaired of finding anything to connect to his primary interest: Mr Avon Barksdale, whom he knew to be corrupt.

Mr Moreland—having more stake in the proceedings, or rather less interest in pursuing what amounted to, in his opinion, a goose chase the likes of which only Mr McNulty would subject himself—put his cigar in his mouth and looked down at the sketches which they had obtained from Scotland Yard. Years of detective work such as this had compelled Mr Moreland into an attitude of complaisance; in most investigations his manner was one of general affability and a charming lack of anything like concern. As he flipped through the sketches, however, he took out his cigar, and his tone was exactly that of a child at last being forced to chores when he said: "Aw, fuck."[1]

Knowing that Mr McNulty would share in his disgust, Mr Moreland referred Mr McNulty to the sketches. "Motherfucker," said Mr McNulty, indicating by this succinct phrasing his understanding as to the work that would be required in order to make sense of the sketches and the heinous nature of the crime.

Accepting at last this call to duty, which was at the most abhorrent and at the very least would prove tiresome, Mr McNulty advanced toward the interior, setting down his knapsack and readying his detecting equipment. Mr Moreland, meanwhile, cigar once again firmly wedged between teeth, bent to lay the sketches in accordance with the positioning in the room that they portrayed, saying, "Fuck, fuck, fuck, fuck," all the while in a rhythm with his work.

---

[1] **fuck**: mid-nineteenth century slang, an expression of dismay.

At the sideboard, Mr McNulty opened the dossier on the victim, which described exactly the manner in which the victim had been found, &c, in accordance with the notes from the sergeant who had alerted them to the case. Over the muttered, "Fuck, fuck, fuck," issuing from the direction of Mr Moreland laying down the sketches, Mr McNulty pronounced his own exclamation of, "Fuck!" as he compared two more sketches and observed the angle of the wound. Using his own person as model, he attempted to decipher the point of entry and of exit for the ball.

As the landlord looked on, Mr Moreland finished his arrangement, using a nub of chalk in order to mark a spot on the floor. The landlord could have no means by which to understand Mr Moreland's marking, and Mr Moreland, wrapped in the complexity and ugliness of the crime, did not seek to enlighten him, instead pronouncing his own private view of the situation, which was—

"Fuck."

After drawing another circle on the floor, Mr Moreland stood and ventured to the window, effectively switching places with Mr McNulty as the latter put aside the dossier and looked down to Mr Moreland's markings. These he could decipher, as though they had been written in some esoteric code betwixt them. Mr McNulty drew out his measuring tape. "Fuck," he said absently, having nicked his own thumb in the process of withdrawal, his mind on the delicate task at hand.

At the window Mr Moreland set up another one of the sketches, marking another point, then crossing to help Mr McNulty with his measuring tape. Holding the tape at the height of the victim so that Mr McNulty might accurately determine the height at which the ball might have entered, Mr McNulty used his own firearm to gauge the height at which the handgun must have been fired.

"Fuck," said Mr McNulty.

"Aw, fuck," replied Mr Moreland, in perfect agreement.

The landlord looked on in confusion, not privy to the complications of the work of detection, or the intricacy of the scene. A more worldly observer, with some knowledge of a .38, an understanding of entry wounds, an ability to decipher the often vague sketches taken on a crime scene, would begin to have a glimmer of what our two detectives have already concluded: that the victim would have had to have been shot from an im-

probable height, were she shot while standing. The landlord, not being such an observer, therefore watched on in some confusion as Mr Mc-Nulty knelt on the ground, holding up the pistol in order to keep that angle from which he and Mr Moreland had concluded the poor woman had been shot.

"Fuck it," Mr McNulty murmured quietly, expressing his dissatisfaction with this position. He could ascertain no reason why the woman would have been upon her knees in the middle of the room at the time at which she had died, and so it seemed an unlikely conclusion. He attempted therefore to find some evidence on the ground which would allow him to more reasonably perceive the attitude of the victim on the evening of her murder.

Mr Moreland, meanwhile, was attempting to guess the direction the ball would have taken from the window. Only when he turned back to study again the sketch which he had placed leaning up against the window did he removed his cigar, ejaculating, "Motherfucker."[2] This utterance expressed his surprise upon realizing, during this secondary perusal of the sketch, that the artist of that work had included a small smudge upon the drawing of the sideboard under the window. Pointing to this, Mr Moreland murmured, "Aw," which evolved to a knowing, "Aw fuck," as he traced the trajectory from the smudge to the sketch of the hole that had been made in the shutter of the window.

Having discovered this possibility of ricochet, Mr Moreland thereupon replaced his cigar between his teeth. He held up the pistol to the window as Mr McNulty had held up the pistol to himself, thus establishing the angle whereby the shot may have issued, allowing the ball to direct against the sideboard. Mr McNulty then approached, verifying this angle by holding his hands on either side of his body and pointing his fingers in a downward direction, signifying the slant that the projectile had achieved through the victim's chest and hip. He looked to Mr Moreland to see whether he agreed with this conjecture, whereupon that good man nodded.

"Fuckity fuck fuck fuck fuck fuck," said McNulty, looking at the sketches and the circle on the floor.

---

[2] **motherfucker**: in this instance, an expression of greater dismay.

"Motherfucker," Mr Moreland opined, in hearty agreement with the disgusted assessment of his partner.

Mr McNulty then proceeded to follow the angle of the bullet to its logical terminus, which proved to be a corner where a tin-plated cabinet was set into the wall. "Fuck," Mr McNulty said again, looking at the wall, for that area proved just as confounding as both the angle of the weapon and the attitude of the victim had been. He repeated this observation in a steady stream of, "Fuck, fuck, fuck," which Mr Moreland punctuated with an intermittent and somewhat more laconic groaned, "Fuck." As Mr McNulty's search of the corner prove fruitless, he turned back to the sketches Mr Moreland had spread about the floor. Mr Moreland, chewing unhappily on his cigar, did not exert himself to move closer, but raised himself upon the balls of his feet in order to glimpse the sketches over Mr McNulty's shoulder.

Finding what he was looking for in one of the sketches, Mr McNulty pointed it out to Mr Moreland. "Motherfucker," Mr Moreland muttered, grabbing the sketch and pulling it closer. In one of the victim's hands was an item no doubt extracted from the cabinet. The height of the cabinet also explained the angle of the firearm; the victim would have had to have knelt down in order to retrieve the object.

To this effect, Mr McNulty opened the cabinet, as it would have been open as the woman removed the object from its shelves. "Fuckin' A," McNulty announced in some triumph, having discerned a hole on the inward side of the cabinet door.[3] As he scratched at this hole, Mr Moreland turned to fetch him iron pliers, which he handed to his partner. Mr McNulty pushed the pliers into the hole, removing the ball, which had smashed against the metal plate on the outside of the cabinet. "Motherfucker," said McNulty, holding up the ball, thereby identifying the culprit in this inordinately convoluted scene.

Mr Moreland took the bullet, examining it from about the length of his cigar. "Fuck me," he agreed.

[3] **fuckin' A**: an expression of greatest dismay.

CHAPTER I.

ORIGINS.

Horatio Bucklesby Ogden was born February 29, 1812—that fact is not in doubt, though very little else about his early life can be said with much certainty. Due to the unpopularity of his works, there is very little contemporary information to draw upon in the attempt to construct his biography.

What few records have survived, including a trove of correspondence and a handful of clippings, suggest that he was born into a lower-middle class background. His father died at young age; he and his mother were supported by relatives in Ogden's early years. As a teenager, Ogden attended private school, until some emergency caused his mother to write him, asking that he return and support her by taking up her relations' (unnamed) career. Ogden's reply:

Dearest Mother,

I cannot believe that you fully understand what it is you ask of me, and what consequences it may have, but I will agree to your course, in spirit if not in letter. But it is not for you to say how it is I will accomplish this thing, or what shape the channel of my life may take. I will assist you, but I will not work for Beckinridge, nor will I apply myself to the tasks of book-keeping at all. My vocation, recently found though it may be, is my own, and it is only my own counsel that I will accept on the matter.

In recent weeks I have increased my exploration of the city; I have ventured into those narrow, confining spaces in which we have designated our "lowers" to live, and have seen for the first time the true face of poverty. To speak of us as destitute—you, who by virtue of others' toil, will remain quite comfortable for the remainder of your days—is beyond exaggeration. Not a fortnight ago I saw a man in a nearby court, lately relieved of life by the wilfulness of natural elements—though he had been surrounded in sleep by the bodies of the other street dwellers. When I first spied him, his confederates had shortly before discovered his condition, and had retreated to a distance from the corpse, which lay cold and uncushioned upon the pavement.

Those poor souls who cowered and only slowly crept with open hands and hungry eyes toward me permitted me to examine their erstwhile friend, his soiled, unclean face; his skin, blistered and cracked by winter or some other condition more common to the world below. The rags that had covered him served to make his bulk seem more substantial than it was beneath; to touch his shoulder was to touch a hock with but a small of amount of meat still clinging to the bone.

Mother, there are many to take care of you in your privilege. This man had none, not even one to record his passing; his friends—those starveling sparrows and linnets that once knew this poor scare-crow, are all as illiterate as the city starlings they resemble; they know not the words that might enshrine the quality of his life, or expose the cruel circumstances of his death. Who would expect me to weigh their plight over your own? [. . .]

Shortly after this letter Ogden moved himself and his mother to London, where he worked as errand-boy for a local paper, and eventually obtained a position as a reporter.

Per his letter, Ogden was concerned with the plight of the urban poor, which had reached large numbers by the mid-nineteeth century. During this time, Ogden evidently spent many of his days on the streets, observing the conditions of life there and recording what he saw. Some of these sketches were reworked and re-purposed as portions of Ogden's later works, *The Corner* and *The Wire*. Though much of what he saw was pathetic, Ogden avoided the pathos of many Victorian authors and strove for a kind of accuracy in his depiction of the downtrodden. As a journalist his profile seemed undistinguished, though he eventually did obtain a position on *The Sentinel*.

Surviving correspondence from the time period suggests that Ogden's relationship with the paper was a rocky one, as he believed the paper's owners and editors more concerned with sales and sensationalism than with truth.

Disgusted with his work, Ogden took a leave of absence and assembled several years worth of street "sketches" into a book, released in 1835. Little heed was paid to *Life on the Streets*. Only a handful of lines in a letter attest to its existence at all, and the work itself is now lost. It must have pained Ogden to witness the success of *Sketches by Boz*, a collection of journalistic work published the very next year written by another reporter turned fiction writer, Charles Dickens.

Ogden returned to the paper determined to write his own book. Around this time he began drafting his first major work of fiction, *The Corner*. It was then that he met Baxter Black, the artist who would give face, features, and figure to his words.

It would be a mistake to say that one creator or author was responsible for *The Wire*, when the illustrations played such an essential role. Just as Sidney

Paget immortalized Sherlock Holmes independently of Sir Arthur Conan Doyle by giving the detective his famous deerstalker cap and cape, so too did Baxter "Bubz" Black bring to life the world of *The Wire* in vivid detail.

Would Deputy Cedric Daniels' nobility seem so stately and so otherworldly, were he not also portrayed with the lanky, lithe grace Black's art imparts? Would Avon Barksdale be as intimidating and yet beautiful were Black not able to capture his panther-like movement, his violent grace? Would Joseph "Proposition Joe" Stewart be as memorable and endearing without his round, peering face and expressive eyes? Certainly Omar Little would not be Omar Little without his billowing coat, like something out of the previous century; nor would he be Omar ("Omar comin'! It be Omar!") without the scar running down his face, signifying past violence, a life of both heroic romance and mythic tragedy.

OGDEN AS A YOUNG MAN.

Today's storytelling lacks this essential element of effective illustration. For one thing, we would not allow our cast to be represented by the "others" in our society, whom Black renders so lovingly. Black gave us reality, and he made it beautiful. The standards of illustrations today are pitifully low, and certainly are no longer concerned with reality, while our fiction demands their inverse, a perverse masquerade of fairy tale plotting nested within a framework of "gritty realism" that is all but real. Movies, television, and the internet have all morphed our expectations, twisted and changed our visions, until we only wish to see the critic John Ruskin's ideal: a pristine, white, purer version of ourselves.

Little is known of Baxter Black, save a few simple facts. He was fifteen years Ogden's senior, and came from modest beginnings. For the most part he signed his work "Bubz", a decision with possible commercial motivation, but that survived long past any possible benefit to him.

The little we know of Black suggests that Ogden first met him while Black was living on the streets, and only later learned of Black's skills. While Black may have

April 16th 1841.

Mr. Kalbrunner,

I find your depiction of McCullough and his environs to be most insensitive to the text, which I have carefully prepared for the purpose of reading, and for the secondary purpose of giving intent and motivation and detail for your illustration. I must assume from the careful organization of the depiction of Mr McCullough's apartment that you are not personally acquainted with any laudanum addicts, or indeed any working men without servants or valets to attend to ones accoutrement, as his incongruously opulent personal articles seem to be arrayed most neatly about his generously-sized, one might say spacious, bedroom.

I was surprised to find Mr McCullough looking so robust and Byron-like, for when my pen last parted from him, his body was subject to ravaging disease – though I see you have placed him upon a couch, revealing his kneck and wrists in a pose most tragic.

---

worked as an engraver—a skilled finisher of other men's creative work—he did not appear to have worked professionally for any length of time.

Though seen as the role of a technician, engravers still enjoyed a great deal of prestige, almost equal to the illustrators themselves. Bubz, however, did not enjoy that kind of fame himself—if the record of existing signed illustrations is in any way reliable, he worked mostly uncredited.

Whatever the initial circumstances of their meeting, there was little doubt through the duration of their relationship that Ogden and Black were uniquely suited to each other both artistically and temperamentally. When they met, Ogden was in the midst of the difficult serialization of *The Corner*, initially released by

Ogden's publishers: Foxe, Warner, and Cable.

Ogden's dissatisfaction with original illustrator Halvert Kalbrunner was doubtless the primary impetus for his decision to work with Baxter Black. Ogden made his displeasure clear directly to Kalbrunner in a letter dated April 16, 1841:

> [. . .] I find your depiction of McCullough and his environs to be most insensitive to the text, which I have carefully prepared for the purpose of reading, and secondly for the purpose of your divining intent and motivation and detail of your illustration. I must assume from the careful organization of the depiction of Mr McCullough's apartment that you are not personally acquainted with any laudanum addicts, or indeed

any working men without valets to attend to their accoutrement, as his incongruously opulent personal articles seem to be arrayed most neatly about his generously-sized (one might say spacious) bedroom.

I was surprised to find Mr McCullough looking so robust and Byron-like, for when my pen last parted from him, his body was subject to ravaging disease—though I see you have placed him upon a couch, revealing his neck and wrists in a pose most tragic. I must revise; Mr McCullough is not a Byron, but some young Keats, suffering from a romantic wasting illness, which makes us all sigh for him rather than recoil in disgust. I suppose it is possible that his pale complexion is the result of this sickness, but that colouration seems rather a result of an affliction on your part, rather than his, which makes you shy from depicting Mr McCullough as he really is. While we are on the matter of Mr McCullough's face, I would like to take a moment to direct you to the line of his mouth, which you have drawn to indicate—I cannot discern what—is it a grotesque mockery of happiness? The stiff rigorous smile of the Death's head? Perhaps you intended this tremulous line as a reflection of the "satisfaction even in the sliver of Sleep" indicated in the text?

Despite the above, rest assured that your depiction of Mr McCullough's furniture is most excellent. I am not sure where he has obtained such stylish furnishings, but they are admirably textured. You are to be commended as to the quantity of lines employed. [. . .]

Black's illustrations made their debut shortly afterwards.

Black's work occupies a chasm between two very different styles of Victorian illustration, having an inadequate knowledge of anatomy and too many weaknesses of draftsmanship for an audience interested in "classical" illustration, and not comic or lively enough to appeal to opposing audience of Victorians hungry for caricature and exaggeration. But whatever these limitations, he made up for them with his nuanced, spontaneous line, and the sensitive way in which he approached his subject matter.

Etching as illustration was unusual for the time, more common for fine artists wishing to make drawings for more limited runs of reproduction, as the intaglio process involved necessitated a separate printing for the text and artwork. (In intaglio printing, like copperplate etching, the inked portions are grooved rather than raised—thus, unlike wood, copper or steel engraving, the illustrations could not be mounted with the set text to be printed simultaneously). Once Ogden began work on *The Wire* in 1846, he was able to persuade his publisher to accept this process by pointing to his great rival Mr Dickens, who had begun employing an etcher for the illustration of his serials as well. Evidence of Ogden's methods of persuasion are preserved in this letter to Foxe, Warner, and Cable, dated 1846:

> [. . .] As to your reservations, yes, I do realize that etching is not the current fashion; nor is sense—nor is taste, or any of the other qualities of which I had previously, perhaps mistakenly, ascribed to you gentlemen, both in the chamber of my mind and in correspondence with writers of greater stature than my own—the fashion. If you are interested in only in that material of which every man may avail himself, may I suggest that you spend your nights not with your wives and children, but in the company of some working women with whom I am acquainted—they are most accommodating, and convenient, I can assure you.
>
> We are, gentlemen, by nature selective. Our God has made us so, seeing fit to bestow us with judgement distinct from the impulses of the beasts who root in the dirt. When I set out in my previous missive to educate you three on the advantages of the etching process, and my enthusiasm for the work of my new illustrator who is quite skilled in the technique himself, it was not to persuade you, to flatter and cajole so as to obtain something that should not by rights be mine: it was because, in my faith in the tastes and sound judgement of you gentlemen, with whom I have entrusted my livelihood and work and future success, I believed truly that were I to set out the facts of the matter plainly and without adornment, you would see the rightness of this judgement.
>
> Do not put this supposition to lie. [. . .]

Had his publishers known the dismal sales and negative press that would greet *The Wire* upon its initial publication, it is unlikely they would have been much persuaded by Ogden's appeals. But once the course was set, they continued their accommodation on these points.

This was not the only time that Ogden would have arguments with his publishers regarding the work of his collaborator. Although Foxe, Warner, and Cable allowed Ogden great latitude in the text of *The Corner*, and later on *The Wire* as well, they were more squeamish about depicting those same sequences in the visuals.

Although no correspondence relating to it has survived, we have existing prints of at least one rejected illustration, depicting Greggs surveying her wily informant Bubbles through her field glass. It's possible that this plate was rejected for practical reasons, as it does not directly depict the action of the scene delineated in the text—Bubbles, identifying suspects by handing out hats.

But the most likely reason for their rejection is right there in the foreground of the print—Greggs' lovingly depicted, be-panted posterior. It was one thing to graphically depict a death by kicking, or a character splayed out on a wreckage of building materials like a cyclopsidic Christ on a cross of industry, but a true visual depiction of Greggs, as she appeared in the text, seemed impossible. Although she is a central figure in three of the five volumes of *The Wire*, she appears in a single illustration only, and then merely from the waist up, and at a great distance. That is, unless you count the tiny rooftop dot in the distance of the actual print illustration of the Bubbles scene in question.

Ogden himself was hardly the ideal collaborator. His striving for realism in every particular caused him to demand complete honesty of Black, emphasizing that all their work should capture not the present sentiment of the times, but the truth of their own lives and experience. This unique mandate caused Black to experiment with style, often inventing techniques not put to use again for decades.

When Ogden needed to correct his collaborator's course, he did so with gentleness and clear admiration.

> Your depiction of the fisticuffs is adequate, and your rendering is as usual fine, but your illustration seems to be entirely of the intellect, and to possess none of the animal depicted in my words.
>
> I met a man once in reduced circumstances. Though his eye was keen, and his talents prodigious, it was his hands I most admired, for they did not speak to sharpness, nor that skill I so admire in you. These hands, though able to produce such loving portraiture with which I have been so lucky to see my work supplemented, were admirable not for delicacy or technical accuracy but for their very roughness, their sore, work-hardened state, and for the strength of passion of which I deemed them capable. These hands I have seen hold the quill, and work the burin; I have seen them produce tender works of subtle mastery. But in my heart of hearts, I admire these hands still for their experience, for their passion; I admire them for their ability to produce not that which is pretty, but that which is true, and real.
>
> That truth is not in the studio, my dear friend, and the lines you seek are not in the books to which we have become accustomed. Your lines are the lines of the streets; your eye is not closed in the polite manner of the masses, but open in the way of one who risks being crushed beneath their weight. Create not in the way of the politely blind, who would adorn us all in frocks and white smooth skin. Create in the way of Truth. I know that your heart sees it; let your stylus show it, that we may see it too.

Black delivered.

When *The Wire* serialization was finally complete, six years after it had begun, things had changed for Black. He no longer worked as an engraver during the day, as it seems he was relieved from the position for reasons relating to his health, and perhaps to an increasing unsteadiness in his hand. Indeed, his final surviving letters to Ogden show mark of this deterioration, his once crisp and confident penmanship now jittery and unsure.

Before his condition had reached this extreme, however, Black related his wishes to Ogden of reworking the majority of illustrations for a future collected edition of the series. For posterity, Black wrote to Ogden in 1852, several months after *The Wire* finished its initial serialization:

> It seems too much to hope for that someone will remember our work, but if it should be so, I wish it to be in the best light possible. I feel that this is the great work of your life, and it is doubtless mine as well; for though I am no great artist or professional in any sense of the word, I have produced art from my own experience, and it is True. Other illustrators I could hold at a distance, seeing their flaws more readily, it seems, than they do themselves; even if their illustrations were of the quality of which those peacocks seem to believe themselves capable, they would have been ultimately in the service of nothing. None, save a mere handful, can write with any worth, and those that can, temper their truth with baubles and distraction, thunder and princesses and unicorns and kindly rich men.
>
> I had no great heroes in my life to swoop down to protect me or my sister. No great reward for my lifetime of difficulty. And compared to those helpless that you depict I am a king among men; I have shelter and food, I have my grate, I have my window so that I may look out upon the street when I am able in time and inclination. We are to those truly wretched poor as a hunting dog is to a fox, though the fox may take it personally, not knowing the dog is but prey himself to the master he serves; and yet I am grateful to your words to show me that this is my place, and that it is the conditions of man and his structures rather than the ordination of God that makes it so. If there is a spark to my poor etchings, it is in the way they touch upon your stories. They take, and I am afraid they all too seldom give. I hope for this you will forgive me.

Black lived long enough to complete only a handful of reworked illustrations, and the last of those he completed show unfortunate signs of the tremor that had by now overtaken his control.

It is impossible now, with the great distance of time and neglect, to tell the cause of this unsure hand, whether it related directly to his medical condition, and if indeed it was this same condition that ended his life prior to the collected edition of *The Wire*. Was it the final result of his excessive drinking, an excess that possibly served as a model for the drunken escapades of McNulty and Bunk? Was it possible that, like the character whose nickname bears similarity to his own, Bubz was addicted to laudanum or perhaps another narcotic? Could he have maintained such an addiction throughout the eight years in which he and Ogden worked together, and still produced so much work of such consistent quality? Is it possible that he had some kind of relationship with his vices that was contained when he was working, but which seemed boundless when unrestrained by his heavy workload?

If we may be forgiven for indulging in pure speculation, it is also possible that what killed Black was that which was most close to his heart, the underlying subject of all of his extant writing, and that which we remember him for now. It is possible that he was killed, slowly, by the fumes of his etching vats.

He is a man whom we know almost entirely through his words to his friend Ogden, and it is possible that this bias skews our view of him. It is indeed possible that in reality Black was a man with interests other than art and reproduction, a man who loved or hated things other than copper and paper and ink and was concerned with more than issues of anatomy and viewpoint and depicting a world of colour with lines of black or silver alone. But we do not possess reality; instead we have history, her pale cousin who grows thinner and sicker with each passing year, and in that chronicle, Black is a man of direct and focused passion, who loved deeply and truly his art and his friend.

Her other cousin is fable, those threads we weave from true experience in the fabrication of truth called fiction. Who knows but what personal experience formed these men, also formed this text—which, though fundamentally untrue, is real in a way that they are not.

From BOOK I
Excerpt CHAPTER II. "The Detail."
(June 9, 1846)

D'Angelo Barksdale, Poot, and Wallace sat upon the worn sofa in the yard, D with his frequent look of abstraction, Poot and Wallace concerned with the very concrete notion of sustenance in the form of chicken nuggets and brown sauce.[1] Dipping the nugget into the sauce, which waited in its chipped *ramequin* no doubt purloined from a china shop, Poot eagerly sampled the awaiting succulence.

"This shit is right, yo," opined Wallace, also partaking of the meagre yet piping hot feast arrayed upon the sofa.

"Mm-hm," agreed Poot, swallowing.

Waxing eloquent upon the meal, Wallace continued to receive approving encouragement from Poot as both chewed in rapturous delight. D, meanwhile, sat on the edge of the sofa, declining the offer of nuggets, as he was not very hungry, and moreover was preoccupied. His eyes scanned the yard as they were wont to do, while his mind was engaged by the more pressing task of contemplating his position in life, and similar thoughts far removed from well-cooked fowl and the cloying syrup in which it was dipped.

Wallace, however, was not unphilosophical or lacking in imagination, as revealed by his next statement: "Man, whoever invented these, he off the hook."[2] To the incredulous sounds issuing from Poot between bites of nugget, Wallace replied, "He got the bone all the way out the damn chicken. Before he came along, niggers been chewin' on drumsticks and shit, gettin' they fingers all greasy."

D did not appear to be listening, watching a man approach some members of his crew with a sixpence clutched tight in a careworn hand, but D

---

[1] **nuggets:** a molded piece of chicken and various other substances, breaded and fried in oil, the nugget is a result of industrialization. Mc—— was doubtless the name of an investor or industrialist responsible for the mass manufacture of the product in a factory setting. Ogden was prescient in his concerns regarding the extent of industrialization; half a century later, Upton Sinclair's book *The Jungle* brought the worst excesses of the meat packing industry to public light. Fortunately, in modern times, food is no longer treated as a mere commodity. Government and business alike recognized food is in fact necessary to the survival of humanity rather than an instrument of capital, and legislation has changed accordingly.

[2] **off the hook:** slang. Victorian resource "Urban Dictionary" references the colloquialism as meaning both "current" and "excellent."

often listened when others were unaware. He listened to more than the sounds of the street; he could hear more than the rabble of urchins or the excuses of thieves, and yet for all that he knew the language of bankers and of lawyers, he had little opportunity to speak it.

"'Nuff with the bone," Wallace went on. "Let's nugget that meat up and make some real money."

"You think the man got paid?" said Poot, looking thoughtfully and somewhat sceptically at his own nugget.

"Who?"

"The man who invented these," intoned Poot, waving his nugget.

"Shit," exclaimed Wallace. "He richer than a motherfucker."[3]

This was when D suddenly spoke, his question a response to the conversation regarding strangely condensed chicken, but also a response to his previous reflections upon his situation in life: the frustrating, demoralising conclusion that no amount of brilliance or goodness would win one anything in this mechanistic husk of a world, and that the only way to succeed was this way, in the yard, with a sofa and with sixpence after sixpence. "Why?" was what D said. "You think he get a percentage?"

Wallace, still consuming the bird in nugget form, queried, "Why not?"

D smiled at this evidence of naiveté. "Nigger, please. The man who invented them things, just some sad ass down at the basement of Mc——, thinkin' up some shit to make some money for the real players." Though Poot and Wallace may have remained in ignorance, D was not unaware of the inventor of the chicken nugget's parallel to his own life here in the yard.

"Nah, man, that ain't right," opined Poot.

"Right?" queried D, incredulously. "It ain't about right. It's about money. Now you think Ronald Mc—— gonna go down into that basement and say, 'Hey, Mr Nugget, you da bomb. We sellin' chicken faster than you can tear the bone out, so I'm gonna write my clowny ass name on this fat ass check for you'? Shit."

Wallace shook his head, seeing the absurdity of D's suggestion, and yet seemingly unable to thoroughly process the meaty thought. Poot looked down.

D felt certain Poot knew all of this; even Wallace could not be una-

---

[3] **motherfucker**: slang, in this case "a very rich person."

ware of the workings of the world, as he experienced the hardships of it daily—and yet, for Wallace, there still existed some idyllic scheme outside of the meagre sphere they called their own. Through this scheme, those who worked with honest effort and intelligence, and applied themselves to earnest toil, were rewarded for their contributions to the world. For Wallace, the current structure in which they acted—this system of cowardice and cruelty—of power built by the strength of one's fists and one's willingness towards violence—was the sham, and the rosy dream of some honest system beyond was truth. For Wallace, there was still some dignity in the world somewhere that was not here.

"Man, the nigger who invented them things," D went on to drive the point home, "still workin in the basement for a regular wage thinkin' up some shit to make the fries taste better—some shit like that. Believe."[4]

Wallace shook his head again and took a bite of his nugget. While he saw D's point, he refused to believe that there was no value in the intelligence D claimed was useless in this world of transaction. There was merit to creative genius, thought Wallace—that was the seed to greatness, not these games of pounds and pence. In the end, it was ingenuity that would build a better world, not these masters of manufacturing. "Still had the idea," Wallace pointed out.

For a moment, D merely looked at Wallace. It was then that he knew Wallace would not last long.

Wallace chewed his nugget. D looked out at the yard.

---

[4] **fries:** another example of an industrial food product somewhat resembling sliced potatoes baked or fried in oil: potatoes served in the French manner. Due to the health risks associated with mass consumption of fried products, "fries" have similarly gone out of fashion, though in England "chips" are served as a classic dish.

CHAPTER II.

CLASS.

The Wire began syndication in 1846, and was published in 60 installments over the course of six years, each installment running for 30 pages and costing a single shilling.

Though circumstances make the parallel regrettable, Ogden's work is best understood through comparison with the work of his contemporary and rival, Charles Dickens. In addition to Dickens' tightly-plotted stories, charming characters and overall showmanship, his success and real innovation as a storyteller lies in his mastery of the serial format. Other serialized authors were mainly writing episodic sketches linked together only loosely by plot, characters, and a uniformity of style. With *Oliver Twist*, only his second novel, Dickens began to define an altogether new type of novel, one that was more complex, more psychologically and metaphorically contiguous. In addition to this attention to the whole, Dickens retained a heightened awareness of his method of publication. Each installment contained a series of elements engineered to give the reader the satisfaction of a complete arc, a single unified episode, with a beginning, middle, and end.

The Wire, however, rode a line between this Dickensian method of story development and the style of novels in the former century, which were single, complete works, and were only later were adapted to serial format in order to make them affordable to the public. Yet Ogden was not working within the paradigm of the eighteenth century. Serialization was the format of choice for his publishers, but rather than providing the short burst of decisively circumscribed fiction so desired by his readership, his tangled narrative unspooled at a stately, at times seemingly glacial, pace. This method of story-telling resulted in a an altogether different kind of novel.

Though lauded by a few critics, the general public found the initial installments slow and difficult to penetrate, while later installments required intimate knowledge of all the pieces that had come before. To consume this story in small bits doled out over an extended time is to view a pointillist painting by looking at the dots.

And yet, there is no other form in which *The Wire* could have been published other than the serial, for reasons both economic and practical. The volume set, at £3, was an extraordinary expense, as opposed to a shilling per month over six years.

Furthermore, the majority of Ogden's potential audience would be more likely to browse a pamphlet than they would be to purchase a volume set.

Lastly, one might stand back from a pointillist work; whereas the entirety of *The Wire* can only be seen after is has been consumed, a piece at a time. To experience the story in its entirety, without breaks between sections, would be exhausting; one would perhaps miss the essence of what makes it great: the slow build of detail, the gradual and yet inevitable churning of the great wheel of the world.

The genius of *The Wire* lies in its sheer size and scope, its slow layering of complexity which could not have been achieved in any other way but the serial format. Dickens is often praised for his portrayal not merely of a set of characters and their lives, but of the setting as a character: the city itself an antagonist. Yet in *The Wire*, Bodymore is an even more intricate and compelling character than London in Dickens' hands; *The Wire* portrays society to such a degree of scope and intricacy that *A Tale of Two Cities* can hardly compare.

That is not to say that one did not have an influence on the other. *Oliver Twist* is a searing treatment of the education system and treatment of children in Victorian society; meanwhile, *The Wire*'s portrayal of the Bodymore schools is a similar indictment, featuring Oliver-like orphans such as "Dukie" and the fatherless Michael, and criminal activity forced upon children through Fagin-like scheming. Yet while it's possible Ogden took a cue from Dickens in his choice to condemn educational institutions, *The Wire* builds from the simplicity of *Oliver Twist*, complicating the subject with a nuance and attention to detail that Dickens seldom achieved.

In fact, Dickens, in later novels—which incriminate fundamental social institutions such as government (*Little Dorrit*), the justice system (*Bleak House*), and social class (*A Tale of Two Cities*, among others)—seems to have been influenced by *The Wire*. This is evidenced by the increased complexity of Dickens' novels, which, instead of following the rollicking adventures of one roguish but endearing protagonist, rather seek to build a complete picture of society. Instead of driving a linear plot forward, Dickens, in *A Tale of Two Cities* and *Bleak House*, seeks to unfold the narrative outward, gradually uncovering different intersecting mechanisms of a socially complex world.

While Dickens is praised for these attempts, *The Wire* works to many of the same ends, and does so with more skill. For one, *The Wire* seems more attuned to the nuances and implacability of the class system. Who could forget "Bubbles," the lovable drifter; Stringer Bell, the criminal lumpen with pretentions to the bourgeoisie; or Bodie, who, despite lack of education or Victorian "good breeding," is seen reading and enjoying the likes of Jane Austen? Yet these portrayals of the "criminal element" always maintain a certain realism. We never descend into the divisions of "loveable rogues" and purely evil villains of which Dickens makes such effective use. Odgen's Bodie, an adult who uses children to perpetrate criminal activity, is not a caricature of evil in the mode of Dickens' Fagin the Jew.

* * *

For a modern audience to appreciate the The Wire, it is important to understand the impact the Industrial Revolution had on class in Victorian society. The Industrial Revolution began inauspiciously, with the use of steam-powered, mechanized looms. Over the next hundred years, the power of steam was harnessed, factories sprang up, and manufacturing gradually became industrialized.

Once the Industrial Revolution began to sweep across Europe, the bourgeoisie and working classes made great strides in independence. The bourgeoisie increased in size and power as they cashed in on manufactured goods. Jobs for the unskilled laborer were suddenly plentiful, and lower classes moved *en masse* from agricultural jobs in the country to factories in urban districts.

With the stranglehold of the aristocracy broken, the idea of an inherent equality among men gained some currency, and along with it attendant ideas of class mobility. Any man could be self-reliant and independent, and by his own means rise to power. These ideals led to an alliance of a kind between the working and middle classes against the aristocracy. The currency of the feudal system was land, that which could only be brought through birth. Under capitalism, the currency of power was money, and money could be earned by anyone.

The Reform Act of 1832 ended the exclusive power of English landowners, enlarging the franchise and essentially give the middle class the vote. As a result, the upper middle class kept getting richer: a large influx of *nouveau riche* brushed up against Old Money. At the same time, the middle class itself was stratified between upper middle class manufacturers who profited from the sudden boom of industry, and the yeoman style hand weavers, shop keepers, and small businessmen. These were the poverty-stricken, lower-middle class of which Dickens often wrote.

Meanwhile, a strong proletariat had emerged with the growth of cities, but were not at all supported by the Reform Act, in which men still had to own some property to vote. Yet the ideals of equality of man were still propounded by the bourgeoisie, and theoretically, it was possible that a member of the lower class could become educated and wealthy enough to move up through ranks in society. Thus, the stratification of the middle class and the previous alliance between the bourgeoisie and the proletariat meant that while classism was still very much in play, class distinctions were harder to make.

And yet, those distinctions still existed. The aristocracy had a value system built on history and tradition in which the new bourgeoisie had no part, while at the same time the bourgeoisie were moving in similar spheres due to the money they were making.

All of this is to say that a man like D'Angelo Barksdale is very much caught up in class concerns central to the time, but that his position in society is very murky. His family has shot up through illegitimate means into the position of bourgeoisie merchants, yet he is in essence a working man. His worth in pounds, however, puts him on par with the upper class, a social stratosphere in which he is in some ways unequipped to move, as demonstrated by this excerpt from Book One:

From BOOK I
Excerpt CHAPTER V. "The Pager."
(June 30, 1846)

D'Angelo and Donette left the opera at the interval, for D knew that one certainly did not watch operas in full, if one knew anything at all. They were amply provided full view of the pit below them by means of their box seats, which also gave them to see other patrons in their stalls. The house, D noticed, was about half full, and only then did he begin to think that he had not been in complete possession of the facts. As he and other patrons exited their boxes for promenades in the foyer, he became certain of it: one did not leave early, but arrive late, for there were more patrons in the foyer, newly arrived.

Donette disagreed that this must be the case, contending that if one saw the beginning, one might guess the end, but that if one came in part way through one would not divine the plot; it would be all confusion. D, immediately grasping his error—though it had not occurred to him before—tried to explain that this was in some ways precisely the point; to arrive half-way through was to demonstrate that the plot itself hardly mattered. Those who had subscriptions were already familiar with the themes and characters; no doubt the gentlemen occupied themselves during the first act by going to clubs or races, while the ladies readied themselves for the evening, and took tea.

It occurred to D that the *habitué* only attended the opera at all in order to see and be seen; his glass was not directed toward the stage, but towards others of his acquaintance. This was the very reason for D's attendance, and yet he had been taken in by the opera itself, preoccupied by the great wave of sound that came cresting to the box. Donette, too, had been engrossed by the spectacle, though her interest had tended more toward the gowns of the players than the story itself. Afterwards, D did not see fit to inform her that the finery on-stage was all ostentation, the ornaments and cut stones of no value whatsoever, the cast ill-bred despite their prodigious talent, for he felt rather sensitive on the topic; besides which, he felt that Donette would not understand.

Furthermore, he resented that the other subscribers did not appear enchanted by the spectacle, for he was rather fond of the plot, which he had made out from the libretto. It portrayed a lord's manservant who later finds that he is of noble birth, but D could see why this would be of no particular interest to the other subscribers, who not only knew the story and did not care for it, but also need never worry about their boxes being filled.

Meanwhile, D had not known to buy a subscription, and only managed to obtain an order for Donette and himself upon good fortune—the patron of Box Five having died, and no one having come forth to buy up the subscription. Donette was of the opinion that he might have persuaded the house manager into arranging better seating for them, for she had seen the other empty boxes; however, D had been chagrined enough by his ignorance and the attitude of the impresario that he had not been willing to put up protest, instead resolving to buy a subscription as soon as possible so as not to be embarrassed in the future—just as soon as he found out how to do so.

It was with a similar attitude that D left the opera: he was indisposed to copy the behaviour of a gentleman so as to seem but a facsimile; he had resolved to leave during the second half and so he and Donette left, even though his resolution had been based upon a misapprehension of that very behaviour of a gentleman he was disinclined to recreate, and despite the fact that he would have liked to have seen the ending of the opera. By then D was too frustrated to see and be seen in that box of a dead man, and therefore he newly determined to carry out his initial plan, which was to stop by the tea rooms at Greene's, and then promenade along the Embankment, where gentlemen and women were known to take evening strolls and turns in their carriages, and men rode horses during daylight hours.

Greene's was a fine establishment with mullioned windows and parquet floors; D had never been there before, but they spoke of it at the club. It was still crowded, despite D having got the proper time for arriving at an opera backward, but the host found them a table, and it was not the table of a dead patron no one had reserved at the price of forty pounds per annum. Still disconcerted by that *faux pas*, D declined to let his coat or top hat be taken, though Donette willingly surrendered her mantle for the destination of the cloak room.

They were not dressed remarkably differently than any of the other patrons, D noted, and yet he felt different. They were different.

Even as D and Donette sat in the tea room at Greene's partaking of the fine array of things spread before them, Mr Carver and Herc discussed treatment of D's partner in criminal activity, whom they had recently apprehended. As Bodie awaited them in prison, Mr Carver arranged that he should appear amicable and trustworthy to the felon, while Herc should appear menacing and cruel. Herc agreed to this proposition of Mr Carver, while intimating that for his own part, not only the appearance but the reality of his behaviour would be that intimidation that Mr Carver had proposed. Mr Carver smiled in acknowledgement of this jest, and the matter resolved upon, entered the prison cell.

For a moment Mr Carver only stood there, taking stock of Bodie, who was shackled to the table, there being no iron hooks in the stone wall to hold him. Considering how to appear generous, Mr Carver finally asked if the irons were too tight, to which Bodie merely shrugged in reply. Conscious of his role, Mr Carver took the key from his belt and released Bodie from the irons, then went to take a seat across from the felon so that they might engage in discussion on more comfortable terms. Bodie rubbed his wrist and looked with a suspicious scowl upon the officer.

Mr Carver leaned back, arms crossed over his chest as he chewed his

tobacco wad, appearing as though he had not a care in the world. "You racking up all kinds of points, ain't you?" he finally asked Bodie, the statement less of a question and more of an introduction to a litany of crimes which Bodie had perpetrated, including his beating of the other officer, the officer's death, and now Bodie's recent escape from prison.

Bodie did not appear cowed by said list, evincing doubt that he would suffer the consequences of his actions. Realizing that now was the time at which the scheme that he and Herc had determined upon would prove useful, Mr Carver went on, "I've got a partner outside who can't wait to get in here and fuck you up." Bodie seemed at least partially affected by this, so Mr Carver carried the ruse further, explaining that the officer that had died had been Herc's uncle. "Herc wants off the leash on this one," Mr Carver assured Bodie, in a warning, yet carefully concerned, tone.

Bodie, his eyes cast down, seemed to keenly understand the gravity of his present circumstance, all appearances suggesting that he feared the bobby waiting ominously outside the door, and saw Mr Carver as his only recourse for protection from his partner's ill-contained predilection toward violence. "And I suppose you at the other end of that leash, huh?" Bodie said.

Gathering from this question and all the evidence of Bodie's expressions that the ruse was succeeding, Mr Carver allowed himself a small smile. He leaned in, hoping to better facilitate the idea that he was willing to offer Bodie his protection and even his friendship, leading Bodie into a sense of closeness and trust. "You see," said Mr Carver, in a softer, confidential voice, "I don't wanna play it that way. I know about comin' up hard and all."

Hitching his shoulder, Bodie seemed to fall directly into the trap which Mr Carver had so neatly laid, even asking, "What, you came up hard?"—a question which allowed Carver the chance to wax eloquent upon the subject of his own personal history.

Telling Bodie his origins, the circumstances of his birth and the hardships of his childhood, Mr Carver quickly sketched the foundation of his character in which Bodie, should he choose to look, might easily see a mirror. Of course, Bodie would have no way of knowing if Mr Carver told the truth; however, he had no reason to doubt, and Bodie, being an intelligent young man, might gaze upon that reflection and see in Mr Carver not

An illustration from later in the installment; Carver, Herc and a bound Bodie exchange information in a public house over sandwiches and snooker.

only a mentor or friend, but a station to which he might aspire. Whether Mr Carver hoped for this connexion, whether anything beyond the simple ruse which he had planned with Herc was amongst his intentions—indeed, whether what Mr Carver had told Bodie about his origins was even true—would remain a mystery, in light of what followed.

"You know, you remind me of me," Mr Carver said. "I'm thinking we should work something out."

Though Mr Carver felt sure that Bodie was now feeling much more pliable toward him, Bodie retained a measure of scepticism. It was to be expected, Mr Carver supposed, and so was not surprised or disheartened when Bodie said, "Well, what do I get?"

Instead, Mr Carver smiled and moved even closer. "What you want?"

For a moment, Bodie remained silent; suddenly he looked so young, and if there was any truth in Mr Carver's identification with the young man, it pierced his heart just then. Bodie leaned in, his own manner still somewhat reluctant to trust, but willing to take this risk. Hesitating, glancing fearfully at the door outside of which the menacing Herc waited, Bodie's voice was low and tremulous, secretive and trusting when he began, "I—I want," and then turned into a low hiss of amusement when he finished, "for you to suck my dick."

Mr Carver merely sat there, stunned. It was only after several moments that he realized he had been played, that all of Bodie's innocent and fearful expressions, his murmured little encouragements, even his look of partial scepticism had all been a ruse which far trumped his own. Mr Carver felt great hatred arise within the confines of his soul, and losing all reason, leapt upon the criminal, shouting, "Motherfucker!" and boxing Bodie about the ears.

The commotion alerted Herc outside, who—hearing the expletive—burst open the door and rushed inside, attempting to pull Mr Carver from astride Bodie, who shrieked, "You supposed to be the good cop!" at Mr Carver, thereby revealing that he had indeed been completely in understanding of the scheme which Mr Carver had attempted to perpetrate, and at which he had failed so spectacularly.

While Bodie suffered the consequences of a life of crime, D'Angelo Barksdale and Donette benefited from it, having only just finished a most ample supply of provisions, and now sitting back as the tea equipage was removed and the table cleared. The atmosphere at Greene's was exactly opposite of that of the prison; the people in the tea room of the hotel had fine manners and only wore fine things, and no one looked at them askance. D tried to content himself with the dainties they had lately consumed, asking Donette whether she was enjoying herself.

Donette proclaimed that the meal had been "right," which caused D to smile, for the delicacies had indeed been wonderful, and he found Donette's expression quaint. It was partially this which made him unequal to the attendance of business solely his own; he could not help looking around to see whether there were other women at all like Donette in the hotel, or whether there were any men such as himself. He saw a number of fine women in watered silk, and men in their frock coats; afterward they would escort their ladies to their equipage, hung with silk, no doubt, and outfitted with brass.

"Think they know?" said D.

"Do they know what?" asked Donette.

"You know," D looked about again, "what I'm about."

The look of annoyance and confusion on Donette's face betrayed that she did not take his meaning. She rarely seemed able to follow him when his conversation took a philosophical bent, for which at times D was grateful: she could reassure him that perhaps the invisible things that sometimes burdened his thoughts were of no import after all. Though she envisioned the world as an ugly game of greed, in which only the acquisition of pounds and pence mattered in the eyes of the rest of society, at least this was a straightforward view, both honest and pragmatic. Sometimes D even thought she might be right, that the differences which he saw between himself and the other gentleman at Greene's tonight were mere imagined contrariety. Then he remembered the crimes he had committed, the pain he had caused, and thought that if Donette's view of the world was true, then he did not want to live in it.

When she questioned him, he tried to explain to her the affectation of their evening together: how they might dress as gentlefolk, attend the opera and take tea at Greene's, then later take the promenade in the park which he had planned—and yet, they were still different than those other folk, in precisely the way the new industrialists were different from the country gentlemen their bearing intended to invoke.

At first Donette listened with careful attention, but as they debated the topic, it was obvious that she felt he was chasing shadows. Perhaps she saw his self-consciousness as cowardice, or perhaps she was of the opinion, like Stringer Bell, that with time and effort they might raise themselves to the station that they coveted. Perhaps Donette was unaffected by the ugliness and cruelty of the ways of earning wealth, or perhaps she deemed them necessary to survival.

"I feel like some shit just stay with you," D attempted to explain.[1] "Know what I'm saying? Like, hard as you try, you still can't go nowhere."

Donette did not agree. "Boy, don't nobody care about you and your story. You got money, you get to be whatever you say you are. That's the way it is."

As D had suspected, her vision of society was hard and indelicate—that of a working woman, coming from a factory life: not the opinion of a gentleman's daughter. Yet that vision was a kind of dream in and of itself, coarse as it might seem: this idea that one could rise above, even by the material means of capital—at least on this plane they were all equal in some measure, as they were meant to be equal before God.

Though no one commented or looked at him at all strangely, D still felt sure that at any moment, he might walk on the wrong side of a lady, or find that he had unsuitably tied his cravat—all of which equated to a thousand tiny pieces of evidence that he was not who he said he was, and would never be the man he appeared to be in dreams he held most dear.

* * *

D'Angelo states his hopelessness even more compellingly in his penultimate scene in *The Wire*. A clergyman has come to the prison where D'Angelo now resides. In addition to the discussion of Biblical passages and sermons, with which the clergyman hopes to redeem the souls of the prisoners, he also discusses classic literature.

One such discussion centers around *The Great Gatsby* by F. Scott Fitzgerald, a mock epic which appeared in the mid-eighteenth century. Like Jonathan Swift, Fitzgerald comments on society through his work, and like Alexander Pope, he uses a somewhat romantic framework to do so. Gatsby is interesting in this context because the 1700s, the Age of Enlightenment, marked the rise of individualism and utilitarianism, fundamental philosophies on which capitalism relies heavily. *Gats-*

---

[1] **shit**: Victorian slang. In this case, "bad things"

by, however, examines the flaws of capitalism—and so does D'Angelo Barksdale:

"He's saying that the past is always with us. That where we come from, what we go through, how we go through it—all this shit matters. [. . .] It's like you can change up, right, you can say you somebody new, you can give yourself a whole new story, but what came first is who you really are, and what happened before is what really happened. And it don't matter that some fool say he different, 'cause the only thing that make you different is what you really do, or what you really go through."

All of D'Angelo's little *faux pas* highlight to him the differences between his background and that of the other people around him. He can move in an upper class world, but because he was not born into it he doesn't know all the rules, and so feels he will always stand out. D'Angelo's analysis is both a reflection on Gatsby, and on the times in which he lived.

D'Angelo's feelings have some parallels to the socialist ideas of the time: the idea that consciousness is a construct of society. If D'Angelo is formed by his society, he can never be equal to other members of his society, because the society itself is unequal. One of the central questions of *The Wire*, then, is whether a man can give himself "a whole new story."

The juxtaposition of the scene with Carver, Herc, and Bodie against the scene with Donette and D'Angelo taking tea could even, in a sense, address this. In the Scotland Yard sequence, Carver tells Bodie that he comes from a similar background; he tells Bodie: "You remind me of me." Yet Carver has an honest job and is most likely considered by others to be a respectable member of society. If what Carver tells Bodie about his past is true—and is not telling Bodie this merely to win his sympathy—then Carver is someone who has "changed up."

Carver, however, has not made a fortune; when he compares himself to Bodie, he is not offering Bodie a glimpse of a future filled with fine dining, society balls, and a brougham. He is rather attempting to demonstrate that a hard past and upbringing need not result in crime, or violence, or the social stigma of the destitute. Carver has changed his story by walking the straight and narrow; though he might have felt less comfort in an opera house even than D'Angelo, at least he does not need to wonder whether those around him suspect his life is a lie.

Carver's "whole new story" is that he's a "good cop," that he's relatable, that he is a sympathetic ear. But in the end, "the only thing that makes a difference" is what Carver "really does"—which is box Bodie about the ears, becoming the "bad cop."

There are many characters who try to give themselves "whole new stories" in

The Wire. The ways in which they fail, however, are wildly divergent. Ziggy Sobotka, in Book 2, is one of the more amusing failures.

From BOOK II
Excerpt CHAPTER XXI "Duck and Cover."
(July 27, 1847)

    The tavern down by the docks was enjoying its usual patronage of the stevedores of an evening, who—weary after the day's toil—availed themselves of each other's company, long draughts of mead, and the service of Dolores, that establishment's mistress. This tavern, being frequented by such folk as are used to hard labour and moreover, the effects of the morning after a drop, had been the scene of many a night of high jinks of which the stevedores themselves had frequently taken part. That night, however, there entered the tavern a character unlike any the stevedores had seen before, save that they were well acquainted with Ziggy Sobotka and his tomfoolery, which frequently surpassed their own.

    Ziggy, however, had outdone even himself in this instance, sporting a pair of wire spectacles with dark glass frames, a finely tailored frock coat—the fitting alone of which must have cost at the least a day's wages on the docks—the cane of a blind man, which he rattled in front of him, and most strikingly: a long leash attached to a diamond collar, inside of which was the neck of a froth-coloured and most handsome Aylesbury duck.

    Among the jovial incredulity of the stevedores gathered in the tavern, the mistress of the establishment turned to establish the grounds for the commotion. This stalwart lady, having borne witness to any number of strange manner of things got up to among dock-workers, and being well-used to the larks perpetrated by a man gone rather too hard over to drink, was nevertheless surprised. "I say, look at this!" she said.

    "Dolla?" Ziggy ejaculated, in the manner of a man bearing the affliction to which his cane attested. "Dolores, is that you? Hey, Dolores, I'd like you to meet my attorney." Ziggy handed over that instrument which substituted for sight to the nearest stevedore, who shook his head and laughed while Ziggy meanwhile lifted his white-feathered legal representative onto the bar. At this the entire establishment dissolved into uproarious laughter, which Ziggy ignored. "This is Steven L. Miles," he informed Dolores in his most solemn tones, which even while lying to his father, were both demanding and frangible, akin to the tones of guttersnipes and stubbornly rooted reeds in winter, when a harsh wind blows through them.

"Now, I might not be able to see through all the bullshit in here, but he can." Drawing up the leash, Ziggy slung it to the cedar panel of the bar, and placed a loving hand upon the duck. "So, if you will, I'd like a stiff one for myself, and one for my councilman," he went on, to the amused incredulity of Dolores, and among the hooting of her inebriated patrons.

"Tell me it's a fake," Dolores said.

"Well that'd be lying, hon."

"Is they real diamonds around its neck?" called out one of the stevedores.

"You sick, boy," intoned another. "You just sick."

"Like I'm the only guy on the west side of town to try to win the affections of a farm animal," said Ziggy.

As Ziggy himself suggested, the presence of himself in his extravagant costume, and even of the farm animal, should not have been inconceivable to the assembled company. For many years, Ziggy's gambols had been the butt of jokes about the tavern and at the docks. Rather than causing him to become in any way subdued, this constant humiliation had served rather to make Ziggy somewhat flexible, in the way of Indian rubber; he was not hit but that he did not come back, sore, scrappy, bleeding, and more ludicrous than ever before.

Perhaps the incredulity of the crowd, though sharpened by the frivolity of the fowl, in some way was responding to the resemblance of the esteemed Steven L. Miles, in all his feathered glory, to the carriage and character of Ziggy himself.

"Enough talk!" Ziggy announced in a tone of false authority, clapping his hands meanwhile. He then proceeded to order an entire round for the house, by which he meant to include a lush for his friendly fowl. Dolores, who was not averse to a tipple herself now and again, filled a tumbler with whiskey rye and set it before Ziggy, smiling.

"If it's for the duck," one of the stevedores interceded, "the next round is on me."

Mr Miles dipped his beak into the tumbler, flicking whiskey in the general direction of everyone in the public-house.

"Easy there, sweetheart," Ziggy told Mr Miles. He turned to Dolores. "We're going to need a saucer, hon. Put some beer in it. He needs a chaser."

The stevedores had gathered about Ziggy and the duck now, laughing and calling out to each other, more offers to slake Mr Miles coming forth.

Mr Miles, meanwhile, dunked his beak into the saucer which Dolores had provided over and over again. "Pace yourself," Ziggy advised the duck, reminding the poor feathered fellow that he was drinking with dock-men well accustomed to saturation.

Everyone laughed at this uproariously, and the disingenuous Aylsebury continued to inebriate itself most thoroughly.

* * *

Though there have been Ziggy Sobotkas throughout history, Ziggy's uncle Frank is a product of the Industrial Revolution and the social upheaval it created. The growth of the proletariat resulted in unions, which—though created to support workers—could themselves be exploitative.

Concurrent with the development of unions was the birth of modern socialism. *The Wire* can't fairly be called a socialist work, much less a communist work, but the bedrock philosophies were certainly in the air. *The Communist Manifesto* was published in 1848, two years after *The Wire* began, and Karl Marx lived out the rest of his life in London after he was exiled in 1849. It was a time of tumult and change, in England and the world, and Ogden's vision is very much a reaction to those changes.

During the serialization of *The Wire*, the telegraph was in its infancy, barely twenty years old; once isolated by geography and by time, people were suddenly able to share ideas across countries and later across continents. Manufacturing made imperialism both possible and profitable, which brought with it extreme corruption, but also a flood of ideas and innovation. For the first time in Europe, communication and trade were both quick and easy, causing a cultural revolution, as well as an industrial one.

In those heady times, capitalism was building the very structures upon which our cities operate today. Only at the genesis of these structures could Ogden so clearly observe their impact on civilization. Only as the beast of commercial in-

dustry first settled into place could Ogden make out the cracks in the foundation. It is no wonder, now that these subtle faults have brought society to pieces atop our heads, that we are no longer able to determine what caused the chaos; we are not able to produce art or literature which reflects on this fragmentation. Only in the Victorian Era could an artist have noticed these flaws, which—once run deep beneath the bedrock of society—cause the edifice to topple down.

The earlier excerpted conversation regarding chicken nuggets could be seen as a criticism of capitalism: Ronald Mc———, whoever he is, doesn't care about the labor that went into producing the nugget. D references the intellectual labor of inventing the nuggets, while Marx probably would have referred to the manual labor of producing the nugget, but still, when Ronald Mc——— calls the chicken nugget creator, "Mr. Nugget," the laborer becomes commodified; he becomes the product.

Wallace, in his innocence, states the capitalist ideal. To Wallace, if a man is the one to come up with the idea, then he should profit from it. D'Angelo is aware that the producer of the idea of the nugget is only as valuable as the nugget itself—a Marxist criticism of capitalism, whereas Wallace maintains that the idea is not a product independent of its producer. "He still came up with the idea," Wallace says.

While Ogden can't be called a Communist, at least some Chartists—political radicals seeking to enfranchise the working man—appeared to be reading *The Wire*, and taking note. *The Northern Star*, a Chartist newspaper, carried this article in 1847:

> SWINTON—The Chartists here held a small gathering in the Assembly Hall, Swinton, Salford one week ago last Saturday evening [...] A ballad was sung in jaunty rhythm by Mr Harris Dunning, and everyone attended to the latest adventures of Mr McNulty, that literary figure for whom all of us have such sympathy, as read by Mr Adam Bretch. Afterward thanks had been given for these performances, a resolution was passed, stating the aim to advocate and defend the rights of the worker [...]

While *The Wire* was read by Chartists, and though there were politicians in *The Wire* whose characters revealed the corruption of government, these elements were not in any way politically radical in the way of Chartism. Thomas Carcetti, one of the most politically prominent figures in *The Wire*, is in fact rather moderate: a good old capitalist at heart, with some social sympathies—and that, in fact, was the tenor of all England.

Karl Marx was in London; *The Northern Star* was going strong; Robert Owen and other philosophers espoused extreme social theory; in 1848, the face of France and the face of Europe changed. This was the time of Young Germany, of Young France, even of Young England—yet in England, after 1848, the people were not readying for revolution. Instead, they were reading Charles Dickens.

Radical politicians and economists and philosophers spoke of reform in the name of the working man, and yet many of them were far removed from the proletariat. Even Karl Marx was abstract, his work dehumanizing the very workers he claimed were dehumanized by capitalism. Meanwhile, Horatio Ogden, Charles Dickens, Elizabeth Gaskell, et al showed the true "condition of England" by bringing to life the floors of factories, the docks at ports, the workers, beggars, and homeless impoverished by the Industrial Revolution. By illuminating these conditions, and by giving the people in them character and depth, they evoked sympathy in a way Karl Marx never could.

This sympathy, rather than deep political motivation, prompted a movement without much political agenda at all—or, if there was a political agenda, it was that of extreme moderation, spread in every direction. Social idealism did not seek to overthrow the capitalist paradigm; it seemed to accept capitalism as a matter of fact. Instead of seeking to influence the economy or government, idealists sought to influence the individual. They did not appeal to the intellect or to political ideas, but to sentiment.

The goal was interventionism—not that the system itself would change, but that policies and individuals would right wrongs as they found them. A strong component of this was individual philanthropy, which required sympathy. If the upper classes—aristocracy and bourgeoisie alike—could but feel sympathy for the poor and downtrodden, they would intervene on behalf of the needy, or so the argument went. This intervention would alleviate poverty, allowing the working class to access the same benefits as the bourgeoisie.

Though social intervention was not a movement with the strength and organization of Chartism, it was a mindset which had a grip on many people in Great Britain at the time. In his early work, Thomas Carlyle wrote with such a mindset, influencing many of the great social reformers of his age, including Charles Dickens. Dickens' corpus is a testament to social interventionism; his poor, down-trodden heroes often in the end received help through some generous benefactor. Though Dickens created portraits of industrial cruelty and utilitarian greed, his worldview was ultimately a hopeful one; the sympathies of individuals of all classes could ultimately help those less fortunate than themselves, allowing for that triumph of good so desired by his audience. Charity and benevolence—in a word, sentiment—could negate the evils of capitalism.

The Wire differed from these works not because it proposed more radical change, but because it proposed no change. In The Wire, sentiment never gains a foothold in the mechanisms of economy, government, and society. Certainly, Carcetti's idealism doesn't triumph.

What began in Thomas Carlyle as romantic idealism of the past and disgust with industrialist and utilitarian greed gradually became a longing for the return of feudalism and admiration of fascism and German ideals of leadership. What happens in Thomas Carcetti is far more subtle. By the end, Carcetti still seems to support goals of social intervention—improvement in education, elimination of corruption in the judiciary system—and yet, time and time again, he is either unwilling or unable to implement these changes. Unlike Carlyle, Carcettti does not turn to a new system of belief. Instead, he falls in step with the very social order in which he sought to intervene; he acts according to its dictates in spite of himself.

Carcetti is not completely a victim of his time. There are moments in which those changes are within his power to make, but he is stopped by his own self interests—yet the entire structure of society seems directed toward these selfish choices. The reader is disappointed over and over again by characters who make choices that reinforce the current social order, but paradoxically finds it hard to blame the characters at all.

This—the social structure which influences individual choice, the difficulty in placing blame with the individual—this is what is radical about The Wire, in the socialist sense. "It is not the consciousness of men that determines their being, but, on the contrary, their social being that determines their consciousness," Karl Marx wrote.

Just how much is Carcetti to blame for his failure to implement those ideals to which he laid claim? The Wire does not argue that he is blameless. Early in the narrative he is shown to be petty, arrogant, and selfish; only later do we come to understand that he has a righteous cause. Yet even as Carcetti makes bad choices based upon a self-centered desire to be reelected, he falls victim to the structure of government, wherein corruption is privileged, and integrity ineffectual.

This tension between human agency and the dictates of society plays out over and over again in The Wire. The earlier excerpts, demonstrating D'Angelo's inability to escape his past, and even Stringer's death scene—in which Stringer proves his criminal mind-set, despite his attempts to act so bourgeoisie, and for it suffers a criminal's fate—demonstrate both the personal choices and social constructions which form us.

CHAPTER III.

MIDDLE GROUND.

The following excerpt, from Chapter 36 of Book Three, "Middle Ground," demonstrates the exploration of class and identity in *The Wire*, while conveying the challenges and rewards of the serial format. As stated above, one of the issues readership of *The Wire* faced was the multiplicity of plot lines and size of the cast, which made late entry into the serial difficult.

For those not familiar with the plot, Stringer Bell is a crook seeking to become a respectable manufacturer and land-holder by his ill-gotten means. Avon Barksdale is his one-time partner in crime. Now in competition, they have each secretly taken the final steps towards respective betrayal of one another.

Meanwhile, "Bunny" Colvin, a well-meaning policeman at the end of his tether, and close to the end of his career as well, has created Hamsterdam, a slum that the police ignore. Colvin feels that by creating a "haven" in which thievery, black-market selling, indecency, prostitution, etc. might go unchallenged, other areas of Bodymore might flourish unmolested. Law officials have only just learned of Hamsterdam, including the Honourable Thomas Carcetti, who is a councillor being considered for chief magistrate. Lastly, Cutty Wise is a former street thug who reformed and founded a boy's club for street children.

Note the ambiguous moral stance of the narrator and the lack of exaggeration and caricature in the characterization. Avon and Stringer are criminals, and yet they are portrayed with obvious humanity. Hamsterdam itself epitomizes the moral questions that make *The Wire* singular.

From BOOK III
Excerpt CHAPTER XXXVI. "Middle Ground"
(December 12, 1848)

"And all are promised safety from that great and terrible Adversary,
When lightning splits burden'd air and thunder, tireless, rolls;
In exchange does Man guard that smoky chamber, to keep the Devil
Way down in the hole."
THOMAS WAITS[1]

[. . .] Having finished their cigars, Avon and Stringer were topping off another brandy, discussing first the food that together they had enjoyed, and then their fine accommodation. "Damn, man, I miss this crib already," Avon ejaculated.[2]

He was determined to enjoy himself this evening, perhaps grown expansive as a result of the quantity of brandy they had consumed, more likely having grown regretful over what must come to pass. Thinking of Marlo and of Stringer, Avon recalled the things of which he had dreamed when he was young. While they had both aspired to be powerful in adulthood, Stringer had spoken of a home in the country, where he might ride out at a gallop, and hunt any time he wished, and the tenants always called him Mr Bell. Stringer spoke of factories now, industry and railroads, but in their youth his head had been full of summer balls and shooting parties,

---

[1] Excerpts from the poem "Way Down in the Hole" by poet Thomas Waits mark the beginning of every installment. Minor differences in punctuation from volume to volume of *The Wire* suggest that Ogden was working from various versions of the poem; at least five different published versions are known to exist. The first published version appeared in *Franks Wild Years*, a collection of Waits' poetry. Waits, a Romantic poet who worked in a style similar to that of William Blake, continued to produce work even into the Victorian Era. Like Blake, Waits' poetry was not ecclesiastical, although it sometimes included religious themes, as in "Way Down in the Hole." Waits was alive at the time of *The Wire*'s syndication, and most likely gave his permission for the poem to be used as an epigraph.

[2] **crib**: lang for "house" or "home." Avon appears to live in an equivalent of Mayfair.

an attentive staff and twenty families with whom to dine. Avon had never had the heart to tell his friend that the very thought of the country bored him, and no doubt the reality would have bored Stringer as well; they were never made for such lives of ease, and furthermore, Avon did not want it.

Instead of examining these differences, Avon steered their discourse to those early days, in which their ambitions had been alike in the manner of a matched set of horses, who travelled together for a time, but may be brought off to different stables at the end of journey. They fell to reminiscing, recalling fine gentlemen in their silk hats, the curricles with fine equipage; they remembered scampering after such men in hopes of slitting a burgeoning pocket, even following them to their fine homes. They remembered the tall white houses, away from which servants shooed them with brooms, and clean streets in which no derelict vagrants sought warmth on stoops or in the corners.

Laughing, they both summoned forth the memories of their various capers. "And then there was that one time," Avon said, referring to an incident at a gentleman's club; Stringer knew exactly the time Avon meant. Avon had not at all been interested in anything in the club except the valuable items: the silver and the crystal, but Stringer's eye had been caught by the croquet hoops and mallets. Avon had warned Stringer not to take the set, for use of it had been entirely out of the question: they had had no yard. Stringer laughed, remembering the incident, acknowledging his own ridiculousness.

"You were like, 'Yo, that white boy ain't gonna jump over that counter and come chase after me'," Avon said, reminiscing.

"Sure did though," said Stringer.

Avon made a long wooshing sound, imitating the boy who had found them in the club.

"I was like, 'What the fuck?'," Stringer recalled.

Graphically, Avon described the man chasing Stringer. "Your ass was running too," he went on, imitating the young Stringer, much to the amusement of the elder, "fast as you could, punching yourself in the chest, looking all mad and shit." Avon laughed. "That shit's crazy, man."

These were only recollections, however: phantasms without weight or colour or material worth. It was not long before String was recalled to the physical world laid out before them, upon which a price might easily be fixed.

"Forget about that for a while," said Avon, when Stringer identified all of which he might be master now, with his current fortune. "Just dream with me."

"We ain't gotta dream no more," said Stringer. "We got real shit now, real estate we can touch."

It was Stringer who had always dreamed abstractly; he had dreamed of rising higher than his station, and yet he thought that if he merely amassed enough objects he might do so. Avon had only ever wanted something real, something to hold: the funds he had given Cutty earlier this afternoon so that he might establish his charity; this accommodation so well situated by the park where he might partake of brandy of an evening with an old friend; the means to keep himself, his sister and his nephew in the manner to which they had become accustomed.

Stringer had killed Avon's nephew and turned his sister against him, and still Stringer seemed to imagine that the objects in his possession might function as a stairwell, that he might climb to glorious heights supported by the solid bulk of buildings, land, and contracts. The essential difference between them was this: Stringer believed one climbed upon material possessions to obtain dreams; Avon knew one must step on dreams to obtain material possessions.

Stringer had trod upon friendship and on trust, had trampled justice and placed his foot firmly in the face of love, and he had not done so with subtlety. Stringer Bell did not stalk lightly within the minds of men, never comprehending their niceness nor their delicacy; the essential human propensities toward fervour and filth evaded completely his neatly ordered world in which wealth bought happiness, and persuasion came at the end of a fist. Of such a man another Sir Clay Davis could always take advantage; to such a man it seemed ridiculous that judgement should be borne in the hands of Omar Little; and for such a man, that betrayal should come from the quarter of he who had been already betrayed was not inevitable, but unexpected.

Stringer Bell now possessed a yard. The problem he had not addressed—had, indeed, never once considered—was that he did not know how to play croquet.

The clink of Stringer's glass upon the balustrade interrupted Avon's reverie. "I can't get too fucked up tonight," came Stringer's voice, and he expounded upon his plans for the morrow, explaining his appointment with the developer at the building site of the rookery.[3]

Avon inquired as to the time of the meeting. Stringer, though he stuttered, disproved his earlier words: one of them, at least, still dreamt. Just as he did not see how that which could be touched could crumble, nor did he see that the things which could not be touched were the very things which must be built. No doubt he thought the destruction of such an edifice would furnish some warning, emitting a cautionary creaking or a distant rumble in the wake of its demolition.

There were days that Avon Barksdale longed to go back to sleep, to the days of faith and pick-pocketing in sunshine, for as petty and as crooked as it had been, there was a kind of honesty in it that there could not now be in this. "You need to relax more, man," Avon said, for even in those days—Stringer stealing the croquet mallets, his fists pounding his own chest—Stringer had been trying to get somewhere, and had only wrapped himself tighter in dreams. Stringer was stifled, and did not know it.

Stringer merely looked at him strangely. "When the time is right, I will," he said, "You know I don't take my work too seriously."

Wake up, Avon wanted to tell him, but instead replied to his erstwhile friend evenly, even as the dust of destruction billowed back unseen behind them.

"That's right. It's just business," said Avon. Business was betrayal; he never pretended that business was a building contract. Ignoring Stringer's look, which was disturbed as though he heard hints of dawn in the midst of slumber, Avon took a large sip of brandy. Thus fortified, he announced, "Us, motherfucker," in toast, and meant it, even if it was a toast to a dream he no longer dreamed.[4]

"Us," Stringer agreed.

They shook on it firmly, and thereupon embraced, clasping arms and Avon thumping his friend soundly on the back. Then Stringer left and Avon reclaimed his brandy, staring after Stringer and remembering those halcyon days when they had had neither brandy nor building contracts;

---

[3] **fucked up**: intoxicated.

[4] **motherfucker**: in this instance, "friend" or "chum."

everything had been survival, which was just. Nothing at all had been business between them.

Avon did not sleep that night, and yet he dreamed. Never having sought to build a kingdom, he longed only to defend his castle; that night he dreamt not of conquest, but of children.

* * *

The next day the children he and Stringer might have been played under the protection of Cutty's carriage-house, amply refurbished by means of Avon's own pocket, and yet Avon was unable to share their victories, nor their mock challenge to their rivals. In accordance with the wishes of Spider and the other boys, Cutty had asked the schoolmaster at Scrapthy's Hall whether the children of that establishment might be willing to engage in some small contest for sport.

Although Avon's patronage might eventually earn the establishment some measure of respectability, Cutty's carriage-house was not at all to the standard of many a boxing saloon such as gentlemen frequented. Nor was Cutty the sort of publican with any aims in such a direction. Instead, Cutty was content to see that his boys learned their science well, which he hoped might prevent them from learning a different kind of violence in the gutter or the street. Thus it was with very little concern for the loss of sovereigns that Cutty witnessed the defeat of his boys.

His opponent having soundly bested him, Spider crawled out from between the ropes, whereupon Cutty clapped him on the shoulder. This being an amateur venture between boys, there was no kneeman, nor a bottleman; there was only Cutty to assure that Spider was unhurt, which Spider presently affirmed.

Then Cutty's gaze swept the expanse of the carriage-house, which but for the bout was clear of patrons this afternoon, and selected the next pair. Ditty was bound to be as scientific or more so than Andre, coming from the same Scrapthy's stock, but Justin was long in reach and strong. Moreover, Cutty secretly hoped that what Justin lacked in science, he possessed in heart: he did not have the training and skills of the Scrapthy boys, but he had determination. While it would not prove enough to win the match, Justin might at least prove an awkward customer, and so Cutty called him up.

Justin, either having observed the considerable science of the Scrapthy boys or else perceived the diminutive size of Ditty, looked at Cutty incredulously. "I'm calling your name, boy," Cutty said, causing Justin to shake his head and enter the ring. Justin, having lived by tooth and nail, would not see Ditty as competition, and yet it was that very life—that of constant hunger and homelessness—that would present difficulty here. The challenge was not Ditty himself, but the application of learning in honest effort.

"Alright," said Cutty, "we gonna have three two-minute rounds. Watch the low blows."

Ditty and Justin touched mufflers in the sign of gentleman's agreement. The bell rang, and the bout commenced, whereupon it immediately became evident that heart was no match in the face of science, for Ditty danced even more effectively than Andre, and Justin was all confusion. Cutty called out advice, louder and with more scientific authority than Justin's friends or the boys from Scrapthy's, who were calling too, but it was to no effect. Justin largely ignored their instruction; whether he did so out of defiant pride or sheer inability also appeared to be made manifest when Ditty delivered a blow squarely to Justin's stomach. Justin, clearly not having anticipated the present turn of events, proved incapable of fencing the punishment. It was all up, for Justin doubled over. Muttering an oath, Cutty called for the bell to be rung.

"That was a short two minutes," Ditty called out, with the ready aplomb which characterized many of the Scrapthy boys.

"Yeah, I know," said Cutty, and turned to Justin. "Get you some water, boy, and spit it out," he told him, for he never allowed the boys to fortify themselves with brandy. A volunteer acted as bottleman, and Cutty verified Justin's condition.

"Dizzy," Justin confessed.

"That's why I keep on telling you. You got to breathe, boy," said Cutty. "You had enough?"

Justin lifted his mufflers. "No," he said, "I'm good."

Cutty signaled for the bell to be rung again, and they commenced the second, in which Justin took further punishment.

There are poets that have been enamoured of pugilism, and justly so, for poetry is that release of passion which is bound by form. If the whole

torrent of Beauty, Love, and Honour can be cordoned off in fourteen lines of equal measure, with a rhyme upon the feet, then so can Hate, Sin, and Squalor be staged on a floor strewn with sawdust delineated by means of rope, where bouts occur in three minute rounds, and no blows below the belt are permitted. This endeavor, so say some, puts to practice that brutality that is essential to our nature, but which human dignity—nay, even destiny—should seek to overcome. This pursuit, so claim the fanatical, encourages that violence we so abhor in humanity. To this, humanity makes this response: "Not only do we love this sport; we require it. Not only do we require this sport, but we love it. It is a part of us, and we are a part of it. It is our bodies that engage in it, but it is our spirits which yearn for it."

To what do ten or twenty rounds, of three minutes a-piece, owe such passionate devotion? Imagine, dear reader, those dark ages in the early dawn of time, in which Violence freely flowed. Justice was a blow about the head, and virtue was blood bought with every breath.

Imagine now upon this scene of darkness and despair, those sages who first came forth and claimed that in concert with the beast within, Man was born with a mind; furthermore they claimed that if that noble gift were to serve a purpose, the former must be tamed. The beast did not come to heel head bowed; nor has he ever been fully contained. Subdued, yet still untamed, the inner beast lives shackled behind bars Man has built within his breast—such a cage as Man struggles to keep sealed and locked from boyhood until the day he dies.

Finally, imagine another race of sages, as wise as any who had come before, and yet having suffered the slow, stuttering process of binding man's animal nature in restraints, subjugating the beast to mastery. Imagine these philosophers, instead of railing against that brutal creature in Man's nature, embraced it. One might expect that the natural conclusion of such action would be a return to those dark early days of violence and despair in which the monster reigned supreme; however, in accepting that demon, they did not completely liberate it. Instead, this second race of sages collared up the creature, strung a chain upon it, and let it out for a fast hard gallop within an enclosed ring.

Imagine that the animal, knowing it is allowed this measured portion of exercise, discerns that if it is otherwise well-behaved; if it is docile and happily caged through most of the day, then at such hours as are judged suitable, its master will continue to allow that exercise which at all other time prompts good behaviour.

Therefore, in order to maintain the possibility of its recess, the demon will be biddable until such a time as the master allows its release. At the time its exercise is allowed, it will curtail its wildness to the extent demanded by its master: the demon will not hit below the belt; it will refrain from biting, and it will stop laying blows upon the umpire's shout or the bell's ring. By this small set of rules, the animal will obey, so long as it may be let out.

Imagine, in short, the invention of boxing. Imagine the problems it may solve.

We have long accepted this regulated violence, when our societies have also long since ruled out the possibility that brawls may occur on city streets or public-houses without the interference of the law. Our laws may forbid pugilism also—those few may decry it—but most amongst us recognize its necessity in keeping that animal within us all most firmly at bay; even the spectator is allowed some release of bloodlust, in the observation of this sport. Finding complete abstinence futile, we must allow ourselves this indulgence; in so doing, we may be better men. Instead of seeking to overcome our inner demons, we have arranged a deal between us and it: we have transcended it, and thereby organized a system in which all parties benefit.

This thought, in some other form, occurred to the Honourable Carcetti, as he walked the streets of Hamsterdam.

Mr "Bunny" Colvin had shown Mr Carcetti the positive results of his experiment, taking him to those other neighbourhoods in Bodymore that benefited by the recess of such monsters, whose violence claws within the breasts of Man—a recess not of the ring but of a slum: Hamsterdam. Mr Carcetti had seen the compliance of the beast in those good neighbourhoods; he had seen their cleanliness and their lawfulness; he had seen people happy and at peace as he had never seen them.

Then Mr Colvin had said, "I've shown you the good. Now I'll show you the bad." They had hired a hackney cab; though Mr Carcetti possessed his own equipage, he had never ridden in this direction. The driver looked askance at Mr Colvin even as he gave the route. Upon arriving at the edge of Hamsterdam, Mr Colvin had told Mr Carcetti that he must witness the experiment for himself; the former had remained in the cab, and Mr Carcetti had gone on alone.

* * *

Reader, I will not dwell upon the ugliness Mr Carcetti saw in Hamsterdam. You have already witnessed its effects, both Bunny's "good" and his "bad"; betwixt these pages, you have followed the fate of Bubbles and Johnny, of Mr Carver and Herc. I will not offend your sensibilities by describing the misery to be found in this street: the corruption of those who prey off the weak, their own hopelessness to earn a different livelihood, those who are preyed upon, who volunteer themselves as carrion.

This slum, from which all semblance of authority had merely walked away, is that very same animal in Man's nature, of which an explanation was provided earlier. It might not be recognized as easily here, for in Hamsterdam, one does not see a prevalence of fisticuffs; nor is even violence the primary currency of interaction.

And yet, our world has grown complex, beyond that initial realm of ancient darkness. So, too, has that beast grown in complexity; fearing the throttling power of our intellect, the animal has developed its own intelligence—a savage cunning, a brutish capacity which neither scholarship nor wisdom have the means to circumvent, for its ways are foreign to thought, and yet intrinsic to our deepest instinct and desire. Thus, though we ship it to foreign lands, or engage it in the ring, does it still yet claw some measure of liberty into our homes, our streets, and society; thus does it creep upon us, insidious and new.

Think upon how it coaxes us warmly and most invitingly with the taste of drink, with which it loosens our tongues, our bodies, our minds—and thus the locks upon its cage; in a state of drunkenness, the beast suddenly appears, fearful and strange, the lie of the "lower" mind given precedence to sit astride the seat of consciousness. Think of the way in which the beast of men's natures creates the illusion of peace: it fills our heads with cotton and machines so that we might buy a silk hat and coach-and-four; it fills our dreams with floating, dainty fairies, whom we hope to win with nosegays and signs of favour. Enough of this temptation, and—as with drink—we fall to sudden greed:

industry booms up oily and brutal, crushing those beneath it, and we let it topple dignity and justice for the sake of a silk hat and a lady's hand.

Oh think, dear reader, of the way in which that creature caged within our breast slunk—silent and unseen—through port and two cigars, as two men, once friends, plotted the murder of one another, and spoke only of friendship and a stolen set of croquet mallets.

Mr Colvin sought to find for it a new sawdust stage, sought to enclose that beast in rope and measure it in rounds; he even allows the use of mufflers, more merciful than those bare knuckle bouts which lead to broken ribs and heads; Mr Colvin laid down the rules, and upon the sounding of a bell, the round commenced. The animal became manifest—now neither lion nor tiger, but that slinking snake which had been used to hide itself in the night in order to destroy Paradise, and the purity of man.

My own pen shies to describe the manifestation of that monster; it can only describe the Honourable Carcetti, in the midst of this desolation. It can show you an expression of shock an awe, of disgust and most of all, incomprehension. It can depict the shadows which flick across his grimace of strange disappointment, flitting light in the form of figures passing to and fro, but those denizens of Hamsterdam will not become characters, fully fleshed. The chiaroscuro upon Mr Carcetti's face is the idea of freedom: carrion birds that Mr Colvin has released, that they may roost and feed upon the corpses of their cages, those bars belonging to humanity, which once were strong and shined, and called by a human name—the soul. This pen may draw the calls upon that street, so like the caws of crows, but the detail of visuals I leave to another pen—for what concerns us now is not this outward slum, but that inward rot; it festers in every breast—even in the Honourable Carcetti's.

This animal, so insidious in Hamsterdam, was packaged most efficiently in Cutty's carriage-house, where the bell rung once again, and Justin came to his corner. Cutty was sure to let him know he need not prove himself, for he did not like the idea that his boys may conclude from this exercise that he longed for their punishment. Yet Justin shook his head doggedly, claiming he believed he still stood a chance against Ditty, and Cutty could not help the wealth of pride that welled up in his chest.

"Drink and spit," Cutty instructed, which Justin performed forthwith, and claimed—"Ready."

"More than ready, boy," Cutty told him, and the third round commenced.

The Scrapthy boys, while for the most part smaller, were considerably more scientific, being better trained and more skilled; no doubt Ditty had more than twice the experience of his opponent, Justin, who was more than half again his age.

Though he had grown less fond of many aspects of his old life, there was one thing in particular Cutty despised which prevented him from telling the boys that the final destination they sought was victory: Cutty disdained deception. He did not think victory lay in groundskeeping, nor even in the carriage-house or Justin boxing, however badly.

Even were Justin to win, victory was fleeting; he would not win that greater battle called life, nor win the inner war.

Success, some would say, lay in the work he had given up with Avon. Avon, after all, was in possession of those things by which Stringer Bell defined the achievement of dreams: the house in the country and a brougham, coat-tails and a silk cravat. "Real estate you can touch," Stringer had defined it. Cutty thought of the gin and opium dens, of generous wenches and hot meals; he thought of the availability and access to each under Avon, and found these thing palpable but also transient. They were as meaningless in the broad scope of the world as victory in the ring. Beyond that, Cutty was not of a mind to consider whether some men did win definitively and forever, for the bricks and buildings Stringer so highly valued, whether permanent or perishable, belonged only to a few. Armed against the science of the world with only a bit of pluck and a measure of might, poorly protected by mufflers, few would earn the opportunity to learn the strength of mortar or of contracts; few would find as Stringer would that dreams were not made of towers of stone, for few would win enough rock to being to build up even a pile.

Cutty was not disposed to think of Stringer or of Avon; he was not thinking of Marlo or where Michael may be. He was thinking of himself and of Bodie; he was thinking of Spider and Justin in the ring.

Furthermore, for all the fortune and choice of women that had surrounded him when he had worked for Avon, Cutty had only stood to fall that much farther; perhaps the aim of all of this was only to walk on middle ground.

Perhaps we are never meant to triumph, but rather to accept that triumph will never come. If this be the case, we must resign ourselves to the idea that the darkness of our deeper selves will never be defeated; instead, it will only ever be contained. Knowing this, those short ventures in which the animal finds release must indeed occur; the question is only, "When?" and, "How long?" or sometimes, "Where?"

War is too frequent and too cruel; and though in the present days, often far from our shores, it is too unbearable to countenance. Surely those massacres of thousands are akin to all the evil once washed out of the world, when floods rolled hard upon it; surely they are some remnant or evidence of that animal we originally sought to subdue, when the ancient sages came and said unto man, "We may rise above the animals, for we have been given minds and souls; with these gifts we are made human, and forsaking this, we forsake Him in whose very image we were created." Meanwhile, we approve of pugilism, even if our laws do not; yet that sport is not enough to quench the thirst of our inner beasts. That wildness has found another way into our streets, through the stench of smoke and the power of the factory, through poverty and criminality.

What release, then, do we permit this animal? Is there a middle ground between war and fisticuffs which will allow for bruising and black eyes, sometimes even death, but will not also carry down the rest of humanity with it? Is there some violence or ugliness which we may permit, which we must accept, in order to transcend it?

These were the questions Bunny Colvin asked; we know his answer. Accepting that victory was impossible in the streets of Bodymore, he laid down ropes. In that space, triumph is as fleeting as winning in the ring; the ruffians and vagabonds who inhabit Hamsterdam only know a momentary pleasure. Any mastery they win over life or each other is meaningless to the rest of the world—and yet that rest of the world, for once, knows peace.

This acceptance of defeat was not shared by Mr McNulty, nor by Mr Freamon, Miss Greggs, Mr Daniels, and Miss Pearlman, who gathered with a great anticipation, awaiting the climax of their own labours, reading the notes and letters they had intercepted or found, searching for evidence with which to incriminate Stringer Bell. While Ditty lay into Justin, the battle between them fruitless and unyielding, and the Honourable Carcetti walked the streets of Hamsterdam, that defeat already having been accepted—this was the very moment when, into the street of Scotland Yard,

there walked a boy in an old baker cap and torn waistcoat, no doubt re-
trieved from a rubbish bin. This boy rushed up upon Mr Freamon—who
was hard a-work with his doll-sized carvings—claiming his tuppence, and
brandishing that scrap of paper which he claimed had earned him the sum.
Mr Freamon paid the boy, and took the scrap. "Hey, we're up," he told the
others, and Mr McNulty advanced.

They bent to examine the paper.

This scrap was like thousands of others brought to them by boys and
messengers and vagrants, purchased from pages delivering telegrams and
from peddlers on the street. This intricate set of connections worked as a
sort of net, each strand a means by which to collect evidence; the effect of
them together, Mr McNulty and all the others hoped, was that of a wire
which would knit together a cage to hold Stringer Bell. Stringer, however,
had always been clever, and rarely left such evidence to paper—until now,
at the moments in which Mr Carcetti witnessed the new shape Mr Colvin
had formed out of his own Waterloo, at the moment Cutty and Justin
made something firm and real and good from their own vanquishment. In
this moment came triumph. This scrap of paper was the key that would
turn the lock on Stringer.

Mr Freamon looked at Mr McNulty.

Shocked, Mr McNulty murmured, "That's it."

They began to laugh, Mr Freamon more uproariously than perhaps
he had in years. "We got it!" he agreed, and with the flush of conquest,
the two embraced. Miss Greggs and Miss Pearlman fell into each other's
arms, weeping with that gentle joy of the fairer sex, while Mr McNulty
was nigh unto whooping in pleasure.

Deputy Daniels only smiled, his eyes lit up in gratitude. They burned
bright as Mr McNulty extended to him a hand; for Mr McNulty's conclusion was evident: this success was final. Middle ground, the no man's land
between the lines of battle, is not necessary if victory is possible. They
shook upon it, and the others bellowed their glee.

At the same moment, another sort of victory was under weigh, but this
triumph once again admitted the presence of that animal in Man's nature.
That beast had been hidden between two men and brandy the evening
prior; it had been let loose in Cutty's ring, and now, at last, it found
release in the shape of Brother Mouzone. That man, however, had

determined his own set of laws by which to regulate the baser component of men's nature; he did not engage in war, for he was not a soldier,
nor in boxing, for he was not a pugilist—nor had he often engaged in
betrayal, except where he felt it due, by a code of justice which could
condemn Stringer only because Stringer had sought to condemn him.
That code to which Brother adhered so strictly was perhaps evidenced
in his demeanor; for all the passion and violence in that person was
kept tamped down into an even monotone, and pristine pressed uni-
form of frock coat and top hat, and a cravat which always formed the
perfect shape of a bow.

Standing outside of the building at some distance, Mouzone
watched the developer, Stringer Bell, and his body-guard enter the half
constructed rookery, so did Omar Little then step forward, adhering to
a code of his own.

"Is there an alley entrance?" Mouzone asked, in his smooth,
cultured tone.

Omar responded, "Boarded up on both sides, so we gonna have to
go through the front."

"That's a change for you, isn't it?" inquired Mouzone.

Ignoring this, Omar said only, "You just be ready, Bow Tie. You
know what I'm talking about?"

Mouzone did. They turned and walked side by side toward a victory
of their own.

That victory in the war between monsters and men was making itself felt across Bodymore: in Hampsterdam, in Cutty's carriage-house.
In the ring, Ditty's superiority was in full appearance, while Justin suffered his final punishment at that boy's hands. Cutty called out encouragement, as he had been doing for the entirety of the match, but it
was to no effect, for Justin could barely bring his head up from behind
his mufflers. At last the bell was rung, gloves were touched, and Justin
resigned to the corner. Cutty clapped with all the rest as Justin touched
his bloody lip. "How did I do?" Justin enquired of his professor.

Cutty could not keep the pride from his voice. "Go on home, soldier,"
he told Justin. "You done for the day."

And though Justin had not won, though no permanent victory was
possible in the ring—and though Cutty himself did not feel that he

had earned the final triumph of life in this carriage-house, nor even in Justin—there is a satisfaction in having persevered and in having survived when all the rest of the world goes up in blazes of glory and despair. There is grim completion in having fought a fight, fought it fair, and finished it, even if one knew the outcome was ultimate defeat.

Hours earlier, Mr Colvin and the Honourable Carcetti had been discussing just such an outcome: "I ain't claiming no kind of victory," Mr Colvin had told the Honourable Carcetti. "I will say, though: I'm glad I tried."

Meanwhile, in that rookery that Stringer Bell had contracted to be built, such that workers from the factories might live on next to nothing, while he grew fatter still off profit, Stringer was engaged in attempting to grab hold of that very victory to which Mr Colvin knew he could not aspire. While the Honourable Sir Davis was for the most part responsible for the situation in which Stringer now found himself, he could not help but lay the blame with the developer also, and anyone who had been involved in the project. "They saw your ghetto ass comin' from a mile away," Avon had told him, and the worst of it was that Avon was right: Stringer believed that—knowing his background, and thus the origin of his capital, and from these two things drawing the conclusion that he would not be able to seek justice in the traditional way—he had been played for a fool in this world of business and of industry. All the while, he had been trying to play the world.

Feeling the truth of this most keenly, Stringer accused the developer of having been a party to the plot. Stringer still thought of himself as one possessed with power; if he might not yet touch Sir Davis, then Stringer must exert that force elsewhere until the pressure built to rise him up, that he may one day reach that high.

Even as the developer began to claim his ignorance, Stringer shouted, "Little man! We gonna get all this shit sorted out! And hey, if the shit don't come up right, one way or another, you will pay for this shit!" and he kicked a nearby carton in order to better express the force of his rage.

Stringer's guard stood by, watching the argument unfold, ready lest the discussion turn towards violence. Though the developer certainly could not help but notice Stringer's aggrievement, he must have been well used to dealing with unhappy prospectors, for instead of meekly bowing his head as Stringer might have expected, he attempted to defend himself. It was in the midst of this explanation that a shot rang out, Stinger's man fell, Omar walked in, and Stringer, who—no matter how angry he had been— had thought of it as a business meeting, still heard Avon Barksdale talking in his head: "You don't want to go all gangster wild, right?"

"Shit!" Stringer shouted, knowing then that the only business that concerned him truly was that business of living. To that end, he ran.

Meanwhile, Omar swung the fowling piece in the direction of the developer, who immediately fell to begging for his life. Observing for several moments this quaking, snivelling testament to human frailty, Omar lowered the scattergun, having concluded the developer had merely been a dupe in what Stringer Bell no doubt considered a vast set of pieces, arrayed as though upon a game board. Such games did kings play, thick among their advisers, moving armies through marshes and through battlements; in such ways, empires rose clambering and groaning to their feet upon the heads of peasants and lesser players. Omar knew this, and yet he also knew Rome had fallen to the Vandal; a kingdom could have fallen for one woman, and the life's blood between lovers and between brothers was stronger than the strongest armies of kings and conquerors, who were only ever men.

Godhood is not won by games, however intricate; the same victory awaits each one of us when at last our schemes are played.

Omar turned.

Stringer Bell took the stairs in pairs, his footsteps the rapid, hollow thud of heartbeats on the unfinished wooden floors. At the top of the stairs, he ran across the landing for the next set up, only to look up and find that stairwell boarded up at the top, the carpenters having not yet reached that floor. Turning, Mr Bell ran the other way, through an arch that connected to another room, remembering that at the corner of this section there was another stair. The loud drum of his feet roused several pigeons. They flocked up on a rustle of wings and feathers, catching shadows as Stringer ran.

Losing no time, Stringer neared this stairwell, using the banister to swing himself around, and into the barrel of a .38.

The revolver was attached to a hand issuing from a dark suit, the laundering of which was precise and immaculate in every detail, down to the cravat which topped it. This cravat was one that Mr Bell recognized, less by

its colour and texture and rather more by the faultlessness with which it was tied, the folds of linen forming the exact, indubitable shape of a bow, above which could be seen the cultured, unamused face of Brother Mouzone.

Backing away slowly, only then did Mr Bell fully understand the extent of the collapse of his plans, the ways in which his machinations had failed him. Only then did he realize that he was not standing in the midst of his life's testament: his great tower, his Taj Mahal, his St. Paul's or his Rome, just begun. For as far as he had come, Stringer Bell was still standing in the streets.

This was the end.

Up flocked the pigeons. In walked Omar Little.

Stringer looked from one to the other. Mouzone still held his .38, while Omar had lifted the scattergun. In attempts to elicit the fair play in which he himself had never been much engaged, Stringer informed the two men that he was unarmed.

Pigeons rustled, cooed and settled. Mouzone and Omar merely waited.

Spreading his arms, Stringer said, "Look, man. I ain't involved. I ain't involved in that gangster bullshit no more."

Omar wrapped his hand about the piece more firmly. Mouzone tilted his head.

Somewhere in all the vast recesses of the human brain, there is a portion that is not given to fear, which survives even in the ruins of the timber of our dreams; that had it but a voice, would sing the sound of shifting feathers. That portion of Stringer's mind—flying, though fate stared upon him from either side of a deep wealing scar, and above a neat bow cravat— that portion thought of Donette.

He did not think of her sweet skin, of her pert, demanding mouth, the way she had seemed just like a child at times. He had never known he loved her, thinking only that beyond the considerable charms she offered him, he had warmed to her merely because she had been D'Angelo's wife; she had been his conquest. Now, however, Stringer saw the truth: she had loved what he had loved; she had wanted what he wanted; she had had the same dreams, and none of them were this.

"You a fuckin' businessman," Avon Barksdale had told him, so Stringer Bell, still unable to believe that it was not coming true, that none of it was going to work, that not all of them wanted this thing he wanted so very badly—which was not money at all—said, "What y'all niggers want, man? Money?"

Omar frowned. Mouzone quirked his lips. The pigeons had gone silent, now.

"Is that it?" Stringer yelled. "'Cause if it is, man, I could be a better friend to you alive."

Omar's sneer was not of disgust, but of pity. "You still don't get it, huh? This ain't about your money, bro. Your boy gave you up."

"It's just business," Avon had said, as they had looked back over boyhood. The summers soaked with sun, and days spent on the corners, an arm wrapped around his back—all of these were business; his life had been business.

That was what Donette had wanted; those had been her dreams; he had been so certain that they were his too—and yet, within his breast, he felt a tightness growing tighter, and distantly he wondered whether what caused it was this sudden forced acknowledgement of his own mortality, or whether it was a far more simple feeling: betrayal.

"It seems like I can't say anything to change you all's minds," Stringer said, still not knowing yet whether his own had changed, for nothing ever seemed to.

The birds still were silent.

Stringer shouted, "Well get on with it, mother—" and was silenced by the scattered ball of rifle and a bullet issued from the .38, and the sun streamed in through cracks between unfinished walls.

The pigeons ruffled, and—the excitement over at long last—settled down to sleep.

CHAPTER IV.

IDENTITY.

"Give me the boy at seven, and I will give you the man." This Jesuit saying, variations of which were well-known in Ogden's time, was probably intended as a statement about education, but it could easily be applied to the complex interaction between Victorian class structure and individual choice and personality, of which Stringer Bell is a prime example. As Avon and Stringer admire their lodgings over cigars and brandy, they talk about their collective past, and contemplate their deviated futures.

Avon is willing to work within an older—in some ways more feudal—paradigm, in which someone of his background can only advance himself through criminal behavior outside of the system. Stringer is convinced he can both be a part of the system and rise above it.

This ambition is what, in the end, costs Stringer his life. There was an idea at the time that industrialism, imperialism, and capitalism made possible: that any man, with hard work and determination, may determine his own "story," as D'Angelo put it. Ogden shows again and again that this idea is as much fiction as any other self-serving story: no matter who you want to be, you are still affected by the reality of your circumstances. This theme is acted out again and again in *The Wire*, through D'Angelo, Donette, Stringer, and even Marlo, a cold-hearted criminal who gathers territory and power throughout Book Four.

Though the first three books are able to suggest the factors that may shape character, the youth of the characters in Book Four allows Ogden to demonstrate these factors at work. In Michael, Duquan, Randy, and Namond, we see children not yet grown into their own, not yet brought into the identities they may one day take on.

The following excerpt parallels D'Angelo and Donette's dining experience, and yet deviates significantly. Bunny Colvin, having been released from the police after the closure of Hampsterdam, is currently working in a "ragged school"—a charitable place of learning for destitute children. In this scene, he is rewarding some of the more troubled children for completing a class project before anyone else by taking them to a dinner party at the home of a society lady.

It is interesting to note how many of these issues of class are exposed in *The Wire* through the lens of food and dining experiences. The various rituals surrounding food eating are some of the most important, ingrained, and invisible of a society's regulations. In the Victorian Era, dining was an intricate social dance. Where one dined, when, and with whom were all dictated by society, as seen in the following piece.

From BOOK IV
Excerpt CHAPTER XLVI. "Know Your Place."
(November 12, 1850)

Mr Colvin, Namond, Durrell, and Zenobia were comfortably seated in the brougham, Mr Colvin while he drove reciting some small bit of poetry by Eliza Day, which Namond professed to like. As they disembarked from the carriage, Namond looked knowingly at Mr Colvin, who regarded him with a small, pleased smile. "Yeah, I'm like that. You be thinking I'm all ghetto, and then I flip it, and mess your mind all up."[1] Both he and Mr Colvin shared a laugh at this bit of cleverness, for though Mr Colvin's mind was in sound order, he was indeed delighted by Namond's heretofore unrealized enjoyment of poetry.

"Next time we do this Mr Colvin, could you please make it on the weekend?" intoned Zenobia, apparently less enchanted by Eliza, although enamored enough of the entire experience in the brougham to presuppose that it would occur again. "I only had like three hours between school and now to get ready."

"Well, you look fine, Zenobia," Mr Colvin assured her, for indeed she did. No doubt her sisters had helped her, for her hair was arranged in fine coils atop her head and banded about with a turban, from which a feather bobbed with serious intent. The vane of this bauble was not at all bent or faded, and was in fact of a most unnatu-

---

[1] **ghetto**: Derived from the commonly accepted definition of "ghetto"; the term was used as an adjective in Victorian slang to mean, "lacking taste." Namond would most likely not be well-versed in the poetry of Esther Milnes Day (husband of the abolitionist Thomas Day), as she pre-dates the Victorian Era. She is even a little before Colvin's time; the suggestion is he has "classic" taste.

ral colour, which did not quite match the smart little frock she wore. Lace had been added for the occasion, no doubt borrowed, but Zenobia wore the lappet with pride, and Mr Colvin meant every word of his modest compliment to her attire.

"I could look better," Zenobia at last allowed, though every aspect of her countenance radiated her pleasure. "How long you think it take to do hair like this?"

Mrs Ruth, a woman of means who was well-known for her ability to entertain, had kindly agreed to invite the children to a dinner party at her house. She herself had come up with the whole scheme of sending the children their very own invitations, complete with her calling card, and inviting several impoverished scholars and a musician in order to complete the company. Her intent was that the children should feel as though they were merely some gentlemen and a lady of her acquaintance whose company she desired for an evening.

Mr Colvin, thinking of the fine things the children would experience and the conversation to which they would be exposed, thought her very charitable, though the course of the current conversation began to stir doubts. Whatever his reservations, Mrs Ruth was a good lady, and the children clever and highly adaptable, which they had proven in their construction of the Parthenon out of wood blocks. Never mind Namond's pocketed pieces; the project had only been symbolic, for as Miss Duquette had explained, they all knew the children cared little for Greek temples or the Sphinx. Those monuments of human achievement were of little import to the poor children, who lived in the shadows not only of industry and the towering rookeries beside them, but in the shadows of their fathers who had come before them who themselves most likely had been thieves and scoundrels. Of what significance is the Roman Colosseum to a pauper, who fights not upon sands or to the amusement of spectators for his very life, but who fights instead upon the streets, for the purpose of humoring human ignorance and cruelty? And yet Namond, Darnell, and Zenobia had constructed their classical monument with cleverness and a willingness to work together, and though they could not be said to possess the education of Greeks, nor the wisdom of Athena, Mr Colvin was proud.

Darnell expressed his longing for, "the biggest quarter pounder, with fries," which he expected should be served for their evening repast.[2]

Namond quickly corrected his friend; either embarrassed for his friend or eager to show his own wisdom on such matters, he proclaimed that the common street fare to which they were accustomed would in no way constitute their repast that evening. He and Darnell were both arranged in their finest: Namond in the hat that had once belonged to his father, and a new frock coat for which he had been fitted just yesterday morning. His hair—of whose length he possessed a fondness for which Bodie had often criticized him—he had neatly tied back with a silk ribbon, which showed the turbulent mass of it to fine advantage. Darnell was wearing boots that were a little too small, but his cravat was smartly tied, buttons shone upon his coat, and to his collar was pinned a bright nosegay. "You better be thinking T-bone steak, medium rare," Namond continued.

"The blood all squirting out?" inquired Darnell.

"No, ain't no blood."

"What you think rare is?" Darnell demanded. "It mean rarely cooked, hardly cooked."

"Rare," announced Zenobia. "Get the blood out, stupid."

"See?" said Namond, triumphant.

"And medium rare, keep the blood in," continued Zenobia.

"Look, all I wanna know is which is which before I order some undone meat. Hey Mr Colvin?"

"Hm?" Mr Colvin had not yet removed his driving hat nor gloves as they walked in the direction of Number 10, Weston Street, where awaited them the dinner they currently discussed.

Darnell, interrupting Mr Colvin's reverie, applied to him for an explanation of the cooking of meat.

Mr Colvin explained that they might merely ask their hostess, who might relay their messages to the cook or maidservants.

To this Darnell could ill suppress his anxiety, that there should be so

---

[2] **quarter-pounder and fries**: Victorian slang. According to Namond's correction, this comment is meant to suggest Darnell's ignorance; he assumes the meal will consist of the mutton or tough meat and potatoes to which he is accustomed.

many people involved in the serving of a meal. He proceeded to fret for the entirety of the walk to the door, where he became doubly apprehensive that the footman seemed to have need of his coat and hat, when indeed the footman seemed to operate in circumstances well enough to be able to afford accoutrement of his own.

* * *

Book Four has much to say about children and the formation of their futures, but perhaps one of the most important scenes regarding children features only adults.

Chris and Snoop are two of Marlo's henchmen. Unlike Stringer or even Avon, Marlo's inner character is unknown to the reader, and Ogden presents his actions with almost no discussion of his thoughts or feelings. His ideology and intentions are even less clear.

Whatever compels him, Marlo appears more cold and heartless than either Avon or Stringer. His circumstances in life have no doubt been similar to those of Avon and Stringer, and without any insights into the character's motivations or backgrounds, even the most sympathetic reader is forced to speculate upon what causes Marlo to act even more cruelly than his elder criminal brethren.

Chris and Snoop seem similarly dispassionate; Stringer's and Avon's associates—especially Bodie—appear rather tender-hearted in comparison. It is perhaps the very frigidity of Chris and Snoop that make the reader finally able to care for Bodie despite his involvement in Wallace's death. What is surprising is that Bodie, though he hates Marlo and is willing to turn on him, does not appear at first to have a long arc of redemption. We only are gradually given to see that he is a boy becoming a man, opening his eyes to the cruelty and horror of Marlo's criminal activity.

We get no such opportunity with Chris and Snoop. They are already grown, and do not appear to waver in their loyalty to Marlo, nor their efficacy in the completion of his tasks. Throughout Book Four, they kill man after man, and leave them in the vacant buildings, the urban graves of Bodymore.

Chris and Snoop ask one of the street children, Michael, to join Marlo's crew. Marlo has noticed the boy's strengths, and Michael would be an asset to their criminal dealings. Michael is reluctant to get involved, as he knows of Marlo's cruelty and apparently does not approve. However, when his mother's lover Devar—his brother's father—returns to live at his hovel of a home, Michael agrees to join Chris and Snoop. His one stipulation is that they do away with his mother's lover.

From BOOK IV
Excerpt CHAPTER XLVII. "Misgivings."
(November 19, 1850)

In the shack on Grip Lane, the small dirty alley which contained a rictus of an old warehouse, split into many different sections, Bug was turning another page of the book Michael had obtained for him on Murry Street for a penny. Raylene was gathering her shawl about her in preparation for her search for Devar. Only Michael was still.

"You ain't gonna find him," he told his mother.

"Why not?" demanded Raylene, pausing before placing her dilapidated bonnet upon her head.

Michael was quiet for several long moments, but only shrugged. "'Cause he ain't coming back," he concluded at last.

Raylene left, and Bug went on turning pages, even as the world turned. They were going the same way they had always gone.

Michael was going another, even as he stayed still, and waited.

The two associates upon whose actions Michael's current direction depended observed Raylene's lover—Michael's step-father—as he stepped out of the shop. Devar was not an impressive man, but nor was he ill in looks; though his boots were old and his coat shabby, he had a fine brow, and a mouth that spoke of some learning, with a well-mannered line beside it. He was fresh-shaven and not poorly kempt, despite his recent time in prison, and when Chris and Snoop approached him on the corner, they discussed such sultry things as what had been his preferences there, his likes and dislikes.

Devar was hard pressed to discover their reason for approaching him, as he had only recently been released from his confinement. His ticket of leave was well-established in his pocket, though he was not at all anxious that they should require it; after all, they did not seem the enforcing type. Still, he was not fearful for his life, as he had lately done nothing to offend anyone, and was looking forward to re-establishing himself in Raylene's household. In particular he looked forward to becoming reacquainted with his family and hers, though he did not discuss this with either Snoop nor Chris. Something about their tone, and indeed, Chris' particular line of questioning, gave him to believe they would not delight in hearing any details.

The details thus neglected by Devar were immediately thereafter imagined by Chris. No one, not even Snoop, could say what Chris envisioned them to be, or whether they had any influence in Chris' subsequent action, which was to direct his fist most forcefully into the bridge of Devar's nose, which deformed and splintered beneath the ferocity of the blow. This imputation of knuckles was repeated in a consistent matter with increasing force in a methodic rhythm which lasted the duration a sonnet or short song, or perhaps the length of time required to contemplate, at the Author's whim, physiognomy.

We are said to possess certain bone structures which give rise to our Nose and Mouth and Brow, those features which speak so essentially to our characters, and define us absolutely. We may strive to achieve greatness or great evil; we may seek to be different than we are, and yet there is an essential truth in our countenance, or so say certain philosophers of bone. Bumps on our skulls speak to madness, and smoothness of cheek betrays kindness.

In considering this science, one must consider the fleshiness of children: not all bones are fused in the beginning, and one will note among some young ones the propensity of the Chin to lengthen, the Nose to flatten, the Cheeks to rise, and so on. That is to say that the child's face is not fully formed, which prompts the inquiry: when may the face be said to be fully set, and are there experiences in youth which may alter its ultimate form? Indeed, Chris' face was fine and strong; the Brow, though low, is not too heavy, and the bones of the Jaw are firm and proud. There was nothing in that face which betrayed the violence of the fists; is it possible some alteration in his childhood may have informed his features? If that is the case, then physiognomy cannot be said to be a science of prediction, in which case we question its value.

Furthermore, Chris' application of this science by direct means of his fist so distorted Devar's features that they indeed became most malleable, which I submit to you, reader, is further evidence of the falsity of this study. If the features may be rearranged so completely merely by repeated and rhythmic employment of fisticuffs, humans may not be so set upon their ways as a Nose is upon a Face. We may in fact change and be changed, by scars as well as by skulls, and by those things which remain unseen.

I have not yet described Michael; I feel some silent exhortation to do so, though he sat in Grip Lane with Bug, and was not witness to that rearrangement of looks which may have made Devar more palatable to him. Michael, though young, had a high brow which spoke to his noble nature. His nose was good and straight, of excellent calibre, in the style of ancient leaders before him. His lips were full, but possessed with that equanimity, that fairness which we come to expect in those generous of mouth, and fire in the eyes. There was something plain about the arrangement of his features, but they were so good and strong in form that there was something striking in the face which was matched in the bearing; he appeared a noble man, generous, honourable and true.

In so many respects, Michael was just such a young man. His most obvious goal in life was the care and protection of his young brother, Bug; towards his friends he was kind; in the face of adversity, he was brave. Knowing Michael, no one would expect that he would commission the violence now being perpetrated on Devar, and yet Snoop knew Chris; she would never have attested that he might inflict the violence now occuring. In his work, Chris was clean and accurate; Snoop had never seen him be carried away by high emotion.

And yet, as Michael sat by the little grate with Bug, he wore no expression whatsoever, and Chris continued to sculpt Devar's, making such noises as are wont to accompany a man having been possessed by an animal, the devil, or a memory. The nasals, which had submitted completely, and the zygomatic arch, which on the left side had been shattered, now formed a concave structure which cupped in its broken bone a mass of wet pulp that did not at all resemble human flesh.

"Damn," said Snoop, as Chris turned and walked away from his work. "You didn't even wait to get the motherfucker in the house." She turned, swinging her bucket, and followed him into the night.

At length Raylene returned to the hovel on Grip Lane. As she removed her shawl, it was obvious even in her mien that she had seen neither hide nor hair of Devar; her reluctance to look toward Michael and prove him right spoke the truth of it.

Michael's fine, kind lips drew into a grin, a smile which was purity and innocence itself.

* * *

This is one of the most forceful and graphic descriptions in *The Wire*. The text provides no direct explanation for Chris' violence, yet the scene manages to evoke sympathy in a way that detailed descriptions of Chris' past, childhood, and home life never could. It is obvious in this scene that past experience has in some way helped shaped Chris' response, and the very fact of this glimpse into Chris' psyche allows us to at last see him as human.

The character of Michael is a counterpoint to Chris. The text implies Chris and Michael share past experiences, but Chris, as an adult, is self-reliant. He has become the person he is: someone who murders without the blink of an eye, someone who in almost every scene is completely lacking in compassion. Michael, however, is unable to dispose of Devar himself. He needs Chris and Snoop's help.

As the two adults show him the ropes of their criminal activity, Michael sometimes questions their heartlessness, and reveals his sympathy toward other people. Simultaneously, we observe the slow calcification of Michael's character. Much of his violent behavior is a result of his obvious desire to protect people he cares for—particularly his little brother Bug, but also his friends, including Dukie and Randy.

In the following excerpt, many of the children in Tilghman School have learned that Randy talked to the police about Kevin, whose death Poot and Bodie were discussing earlier.

From BOOK IV
Excerpt CHAPTER XLVIII. "A New Day."
(November 26, 1850)

Randy, Michael, and Duquan came out into the school yard smiling, only just having been dismissed by Mr P, and reminiscing over the night previous, on which the police officer Mr Walker had been served just due.

It was just as they crossed the yard that a group of four larger boys intercepted their path with obvious intent, though Michael remained calm, and did not let their threatening figures deter him. "What the fuck is up with y'all?" he asked.

"We wanna have a word with your boy, here," said one of the boys, doubtless the leader of the tight little group, for they flared out in a formation about him.

Michael glanced down at Randy, who gazed up at him with worried appeal, while Dukie nervously tugged the strap holding his books. "Ain't nothing stopping you," Michael pointed out, spreading his arms expansively as he feigned ignorance. "Talk."

"You know what we mean," said the boy, for Michael did indeed.

"Yo, that little bitch was talking to the police," another boy elucidated, as though the word of Randy's supposed perfidy had not yet met Michael's ears, nor indeed, the ears of all the boys at Tilghman School.

"That's a lie," Randy piped in his defence. "I ain't been doing no snitching."

"The fuck you ain't!" cried the leader.

"He look like he about to pee on hisself right now," the second boy observed with a little smirk, for worry indeed creased Randy's brow, though a frown graced Michael's. Dukie tugged his strap again.

"You ain't gonna stand by no rat motherfucker, is you?" asked the leader.

Michael appeared to give the matter serious consideration, though if anyone had asked him, he did not require contemplation for the action he next employed.

The night before, Michael had taken off his mask when they assaulted Mr Walker, the police officer who had been bullying them. More and more, Michael was showing his true face, but it was not the face of David, carved in stone. It was no heroic instinct which bid him take up the cause of those smaller and weaker; it was no strain of valour running through veins of marble, but rather the knowledge of his own experience. What made him defend Randy was as malleable as the body of Devar, beaten into another shape and now malformed, residing in a vacant house; that which made Michael stand up for his friend could turn to violence against his enemies just as easily.

"Naw," said Michael finally, in answer to the leader of the other boy's question. "I ain't standing with no rat." Thereby having defined Randy, and so himself, Michael calmly removed his books from his shoulder, wrapped his hand about their strap, and swung them at the leader's head.

There ensued a brawl nothing at all like Chris' encounter with Devar, but whatever the form of the face, the blood beneath flows the same, even from Michael, who was only flesh within.

* * *

While Michael could easily become Chris, or even Marlo, his defense of his peers and his occasional compassion suggest that his own path might be more similar to Omar's. Shortly after this scene, Namond—also friends with Michael—questions Michael's defense of Randy. Michael claims he was just standing by his friend, but he must have known the risk: essentially, Randy had ratted out Marlo, and standing by Randy means standing against Marlo. "It's not that you do shit," Namond says finally. "It's how you do it." He informs Michael that people have begun to talk.

The Wire isn't only concerned with what informs people's characters, but what informs other people's perception of them. While every character is rendered with an extraordinary attention to detail, some characters simultaneously suggest archetypes which make them almost symbolic. This is made most explicit in the character of Omar Little.

Little isn't Dickensian. Nor is he a character in the style of Thackeray, Eliot, Trollope, or any of the most famous serialists. If we must compare him to characters of the Victorian times, he most closely resembles a creation of a Brontë; he could have come from *Wuthering Heights*.

The reason that Little so closely resembles a Brontë hero is that the estimable sisters were often not writing in the Victorian paradigm at all, but rather in the Gothic. Their heroes were Byronic, and Lord Byron himself took his cue from the ancient tradition of Romance, culminating in Spenser's *Faerie Queene*, but originating further back. Little would not be out of place in *Faerie Queene*, and even less so in *Don Quixote*: an errant knight wielding a sword, facing dragons, no man his master.

The character builds on the tradition of the quintessential Robin Hood and borrows qualities from many of the great chivalric romances of previous centuries. Meanwhile there is an element of the fay, mirroring Robin Hood's own pre-

decessor—Goodfellow or Puck—and prefiguring later dashing, mysterious heroes who also play the part of the fop, such as the Scarlet Pimpernel.

As previously mentioned, Little also has the flavor of the Gothic: brooding, hell-bent on revenge. Indeed, there is a darkness to the character that would not suit Sir Gawain, but does not seem out of place in a Don Juan or Brontë's Heathcliffe. Little is in fact an amalgamation of these traditions, an essential archetype.

But life is not all brooding adventuring. Some of Omar's most compelling scenes depict the incongruity of myth existing alongside the strictures of mere men. In the following excerpt Omar appears at court as a witness against Bird. Bird is an associate of Avon Barksdale, who has killed Omar's dearest friend, Brandon. In this scene, Omar is interrogated by Maurice Levy, Bird's (and not coincidentally, Avon and Stringer's) lawyer.

From BOOK II.
Excerpt CHAPTER XIX. "All Prologue."
(July 6, 1847)

The assizes were held and an old town-hall, wherein Omar was held in an antechamber, wherein a pen was held by the sheriff, who was working out some word puzzle or other held by the general press. Within the courtroom, the Sessions were beginning. The sheriff took rather less interest in this than his puzzle, such that when Omar asked some small question regarding the proceedings, the sheriff only returned a query regarding the abstract application of Latin: "Mars is the god of war, isn't he?"

"Planet, too."

"I know it's a planet," said the sheriff, who did not look up to see Omar smile in the wake of this dismissal. "But the clue is, 'Greek god of war.'"

Perceiving then that the man had confused his Virgil and his Plato, Omar provided the appropriate answer in Greek. The sheriff looked up at this, and Omar further elucidated. "Greeks called him Ares. Same dude, different name is all."[1]

---

[1] **dude**: Victorian slang, "fellow" or "chap"

Avon Barksdale had been placed in the gaol, but now there was Stringer Bell to consider: essentially similar gentlemen, who possessed contrasting monikers. Omar had never thought of them as gods of war, for they were only ever mortals.

The sheriff looked down at his word puzzle. Ares indeed fit as an answer, and he offered Omar his thanks.

"It's all good," said Omar. "See, back in middle school, I used to love them myths."[2] The sheriff smiled at him incredulously, while Omar only nodded. "That stuff was deep. Truly."

An usher came into the antechamber to inform Omar he was to be admitted into the courtroom, whereupon Omar stood, reached into his pocket, and pulled out a silk cravat. This he wrapped about his neck atop his jacket, for he had no collar upon which to fit the line of silk, and fastened it with a loose knot. This method of wearing the cravat made it seem less like a gentlemanly ornament, and more perhaps a workingman's bandana; however, the color and quality of the cloth was such that its original purpose could not be mistaken: it was gray pearl, with flowers embroidered in fine gold thread. Throughout the process of outfitting himself in the bit of nonsense, Omar smirked at the sheriff, who was now preoccupied by Omar, instead of his word puzzle. The silk affixed, Omar turned and followed the usher into the courtroom.

As Omar walked into the courtroom, he greeted Stringer Bell, who stood in the gallery and frowned as Omar passed. Then that witness waved his floppy cravat at the Bar, the very same attorney who had advised him to outfit himself appropriately, and who now gave a little start of dismay as to the state of that cavalier haberdashery. The usher having moved him through the crowd, Omar now entered the box, where he settled himself and the crier approached. The heavy, black, leather-bound Book, which so many greasy hands and lips had touched, was thrust in his direction, the crier asking for the truth of his testimony. Omar assured him on this subject, and kissed the Book.

---

[2] The school to which Omar refers is probably a ragged school for poor children or orphans. Gentlemen in the Victorian Era were expected to be well versed in Greek and Latin, as part of a "classic" education. Schoolmasters often taught this material even at the poorest schools, having received such an education, or feeling—as scholars of the times did—that such knowledge was necessary. The sheriff is most likely surprised because Omar wouldn't have had use for said knowledge. Even boys who had been taught a little bit of Latin or Greek rarely retained it, as it wasn't pertinent to anything but leisure at the time. The sheriff himself is evidence of this.

A junior counsel then demanded his name, to which Omar gave a full response in ringing, clear tones, having played witness before court in previous circumstances, and knowing his duty. A few further formal questions were put to him, which he answered as best he could, not being in as full possession as some people as to the number of years he had lived, where he might rest his head of an evening, or how one might define his occupation.

"What exactly do you do for a living?" interrupted the senior counsel, when Omar asked for clarification of this last question.

"I rip and run," Omar explained, for such business did keep him alive, though he would never have said it kept him terribly occupied. The counsel, having not understood his answer, was subsequently illuminated when Omar went on to clarify that he made his business robbing other criminals.

The idea of this as one's means of living, or perhaps the unconcerned, somewhat amused tone in which Omar voiced the sentiment, provoked a ripple of laughter over the crowd. Although the Jury was not immediately discernible amongst the press of bodies, the opposing counsel, Mr Levy, was certainly aware of where they stood, and did not appear congenial in response to this sudden little turn of opinion.

The senior counsel evinced shock upon hearing Omar's response, wondering how long Omar had been at this occupation, to which Omar replied some eight or nine years. Incredulity writ itself most large upon the senior counsel's face, for it seemed impossible that any man might survive one circumstance of thieving a hardened criminal, much less that one should make a lifetime of doing so. A man must have some wealth of bravery or wit; such a career must demand a lifetime of cunning, that the counsel, in curiosity, inquired how he had lived to tell about it.

Omar shook his head, shifting in his box, for there was no answer to this question. At last, he shrugged. "Day at a time, I suppose."

The counsel went on to question him, inquiring as to his location on the night in question, and whom he had seen that night. As he was being questioned, Mr McNulty pushed in among the crowd, which stood on the courtroom floor. Amidst the on-lookers and men of the Jury, he found Stringer Bell, who stood a head or so taller than many of the others, and was more richly attired. Stringer wore a dove grey frock coat, a silk hat held under one arm, and an expression of discontent. Mr McNulty had troubled himself to clad himself in a frock coat and hat of his own, but when he saw the downward turn of Stringer's mouth, he added to the ensemble his own rugged smile, for seeing Stringer dissatisfied did his soul more good than an entire tumbler-full of drink.

Omar identified Bird with a greeting, and the counsel went on to ask if Omar had known him before. Once Omar began to give his answer, revealing that he had served with Bird in prison, the learned counsel Mr Levy objected, and there then proceeded a squabble amongst the counsel over the question. Meanwhile Mr McNulty leaned in toward Stringer, who had not yet noticed his company.

"Quite a witness, ain't he?" queried Mr McNulty.

Stringer turned, his eyes flickering over the figure of Mr McNulty. While Stringer was perhaps a little more finely turned out than Mr Mc-Nulty, no one would have ventured to guess that Mr McNulty was a detective who had been essential to the gaoling of Stringer's colleague, and that Stringer was a dastardly criminal, the gaoling of whom had only been avoided due to witnesses exactly such as Omar—one who was willing to lie before Judge and Jury for purposes of his own. Stringer and Mr McNulty looked like nothing more than two gentleman of some small acquaintance, each with a fob on his waistcoat and a watch in his pocket, each with shined black shoes. They even treated each other as such, with the kind of familiar politeness with which they might greet equals: Stringer would not address Slim in this manner, though he would Avon or even Proposition Joe; Mr McNulty would not address Herc or Mr Carver in such a way, though he would Mr Freamon or even Deputy Daniels.

"Word on the street is," Stringer said in an undertone, "Omar ain't no where near them rises when this shit pop."[3] The street, in fact, held Omar to have been in another place entirely.

"That's the word on the street, huh?" Mr McNulty asked, smiling. Stringer turned back around, and Mr McNulty continued, "Trouble is, String, we ain't on the street. We in a court of law." A different man might have invoked the sanctity of his legitimacy; he might have pointed to the lie of Stringer's sar-

---

[3] **rises**: tenement houses, in Victorian times, a "rookery."

torial trappings. He might have claimed that in these hallowed halls, Justice might be recognized, and Stringer and his ilk should finally be brought down by the hammer of the law, applied with righteousness and glory.

Mr McNulty being Mr McNulty, he made no such claim at all, for whatever Justice may claim, Stringer was of course right. The street, as Stringer called it, told truth.

The street often tells the truth, for it tells stories, which form the frame of reality in a way dry, inflexible Law cannot. The Law admits lies, for it is concerned only with fact, which can be falsified; the conviction of a real story, its meaning, cased deep down, cannot be faked. And yet the accoutrement of story—its trappings—all of it is fiction, and thus inadmissible in court. Procedure will not admit a dressing up, though Judge, Jury, and Justice are themselves a kind of play-acting: wigs, robes, and bands an obfuscation of the truth. There was a reason why, among all the gentlemen attending, Omar Little only made one small concession to pomp and circumstance, and why he did so defiantly, in the careless tying of a cravat.

Law, Mr McNulty meant to say, was a lie, for on the streets where there was no Justice, there was in its place truth. For once, he was glad of the fact. Smiling, Mr McNulty moved back away from Stringer.

Mr Levy having won his point with the Judge, the counsel returned to their places at the Bar, and the prosecuting attorney instructed Omar to answer the question with only a negative or affirmative, to which Omar conceded.

"Mr Little," that counsel continued, "do you recognize this particular weapon?" The robed barrister held up a pistol.

Upon Omar's affirmation that the weapon belonged to Bird, there followed a little series of questions about the gun, its owner and location on the day of the crime currently being addressed this round of Sessions. Having answered several of these questions, Omar felt pressed to wax eloquent, perhaps for the very reason he still wore his pearl-grey cravat in such disarray: court seemed to call for a little embellishment. Or perhaps, instead, Omar still thought of Brandon.

"Bird covet them shiny little pistols," Omar explained, to which Mr Levy immediately objected. Omar sat forward, feeling most expansive, and regaled the court by further expounding, "And the boy too trifling to throw it off even after a daytime murder."

The man who voiced objection immediately subsequent to this comment was not Mr Levy, a fact which would have been evident even had the man making it not stood and shouted it from the Bar, for the wording of the objection was abundantly more colourful than Mr Levy's, or any counsel's, when issued from the mouth of Bird. The objection was furthermore directed towards Omar's overall character than the comment itself, which the Judge would have overruled regardless, had Bird not also leapt over the bar to lunge for Omar's throat.

The officers struggled to pull the defendant back, while the Judge attempted to regain control of the courtroom, banging his gavel several times and advising everyone to be silent.

Omar only smiled and winked at Bird.

It was then the Stringer Bell placed his hat atop his head, began pulling on his gloves, and turned to leave the courtroom, for Omar had effectively proven Mr McNulty's point: there was more room for spectacle in the courtroom than there was in a three ring circus, and Omar could have been a performer had he liked. Grinning, Mr McNulty sat back to enjoy the show.

He was not able to stay the entire day, which included Mr Levy's cross-examination. The first question Mr Levy asked was why Omar had come forward to testify against Bird at all, suggesting that there was some recompense from counsel, or perhaps even Scotland Yard, due to him for coming forward as a witness. Throughout this line of questioning, Omar for the most part was preoccupied by his cravat, which he kept flipping up so that the shiny gold thread might be more visible, and then sliding the fine silk between his fingers as he lay it back against his breast. "No, man, it ain't even about that," he said, when Mr Levy had finished hinting.

"How many times have you been arrested as an adult, Mr Little?" Mr Levy asked, perhaps hoping to establish that Omar may be likely to desire such assistance as the Yard may be willing to give him in return for acting as witness.

Unperturbed, Omar answered immediately, "Shoot, I done lost count. Enough, though, not to take it personal."

The motive of Mr Levy's question became more apparent as he began to recite the litany of Omar's various crimes, thus making out Omar's reliability as a witness to be suspect. There was only one on this list of offences to which Omar had a response, which issued forth as follows: "That weren't no 'attempt' murder." He glared at Mr Levy, who put on the appearance of bemused ignorance.

"What was it, Mr Little?" Mr Levy asked.

Omar did not stop fondling his cravat. "I shot the boy Mike-Mike in his hind parts, that all." This provoked another bout of laughter from the crowd, at which Mr Levy looked exceedingly vexed; he must have thought any humorous response to a question regarding murder would not be met with amusement, but the human capacity for diversion had come upon him unawares. "Fixed it so he couldn't sit right," Omar further clarified.

Recovering, Mr Levy returned the thick list upon which Omar's crimes were enumerated to the Bar. He then attempted to regain control of the situation, reminding their audience that Omar had after all shot a man, by asking why he had done so.

Omar testified that Mike-Mike was a criminal through and through, who not only corrupted others but stole the money he made by corrupting them, a practice with which Omar happened to disagree. Mr Levy only nodded, as though he might use this information to his advantage, which he then proceeded to attempt, by reviewing the fact that Omar himself was a criminal who practised a depth of corruption. Sketching Omar's character for the Jury before them, Mr Levy reminded them that Omar walked the streets of Bodymore with a weapon by his side, taking what he wanted, when he wanted it. "And this is who you are," Mr Levy concluded.

Twisting his cravat, Omar raised his brows, then proceeded to nod emphatically.

"Why should we believe your testimony, then?" Mr Levy spread his hands. "Why believe anything you say?"

"That's up to y'all, really."

There followed another little murmur of laughter, but Mr Levy ploughed on, reviewing as well the fact that Omar was not receiving any recompense for his behaviour. With this, Mr Levy attempted to establish a level of incredulity, that a man such as Omar would come in off the street to tell the truth of the murder of Mr Gant in the lot outside the rookery, when in fact—Mr Levy concluded, in a flush of triumph—Omar was precisely the sort of man who might have murdered Mr Gant himself.

For the first time, Omar had strong objection to Mr Levy's commentary.

"Look," he said, pointing directly at Mr Levy, "I ain't never put my gun on no citizen."

"You are amoral, are you not?" Mr Levy contended. "You're stealing from those who themselves are stealing the lifeblood from our city." The learned counsel had got up his legs, now, and was working up a full head of steam. His wig was askew upon his balding head; he had gone quite red in the face with the power of this just sentiment, which he voiced in the thundering cadence of the righteous. Black robe flapping as he turned from Omar to face the Jury, Mr Levy readied himself for the final testament to the rotting corruption that was not only Omar Little, but that whole world of ragged needfulness and deprivation, down upon which Mr Levy looked from his lofty tower of virtue. "You are a parasite who leeches off—"

"Just like you, man."

"—the culture of—what? Excuse me?" Mr Levy stuttered.

Omar gestured to himself. "I got the shotgun; you got the briefcase."[4] He shrugged. "It's all in the game, though, right?"

The learned counsel turned to the judge, open mouthed. The Judge, however, did not feel equal to defence of Mr Levy.

* * *

In this excerpt, the counsel asks how Omar has made a career of thieving from criminals, and "lived to tell about it." As stated earlier, Omar's occupation is Robin Hood-esque. Though Omar often keeps his gains, or divides them among his cohorts, he frequently states his actions are not financially motivated. After one caper, he even burns all the money he has stolen. For readers in any era, this speaks to a heroism of a kind: a myth living among men, with no need for material goods. The mythic man is driven by more elemental factors: love and hate, revenge and compassion.

Levy intuits Omar's effect on others and tries to deflate him. Not only is he attempting to erase the good will that Omar's forthrightness and charisma might have created in the jury's minds, he seeks to make Omar less than human, a para-

---

[4] **shotgun**: fowling piece; **briefcase**: a valise.

site. Omar's comment, "Just like you, man," in which he equates himself to Levy, belies both the myth and the denigration. Omar is a man making a living. He uses the profits of other men to do so, just like plenty of other men.

Omar's answer to the counsel's question of how he has survived so long reveals who he really is: he's human, living day by day. All of his answers on the stand make him out to be very straightforward, and very real. His motivations are elemental, but also very familiar to all of us. He is not noble and self-sacrificing; he is human.

And yet, we have stated that he is archetypal. It doesn't seem coincidental that at the beginning of this excerpt, Omar is discussing mythic gods with the prison guard. It's not that Omar himself is mythic; it's that other characters begin to regard him as such. The street children and rabble, so Dickensian in their miscellany, always announce his presence, and even as *The Wire* grows and expands, so does the legend of Little.

One of the best examples of the dichotomy between Omar himself and other characters' perception of him is when Omar seems to magically disappear in the midst of an ambush.

At this point in the book, Omar had moved away, leaving behind his "career." However, when Omar's mentor Butchie is killed by Marlo's men, Omar returns to avenge him. Marlo expects this, though, and his henchmen Chris and Snoop have set a trap. As careful as Omar is, Chris and Snoop are very patient, and manage to get the upper hand on Omar. In order to escape, Omar leaps from a high window. Chris and Snoop check around outside the building for him, but find nothing.

The next morning, one of Marlo's spies watches as the police remove the bodies from the site of the ambush. There is no sign of Omar. Chris checks Omar's place of residence, while Snoop checks hospitals one by one, crossing them off a list. One of Marlo's henchmen claims to have even checked the gutters, but no one can find Omar.

At last, Marlo calls a meeting outside of the house where the ambush had been. He asks from which window Omar jumped, and Chris points to it. Marlo looks up, Ogden describing the shock and incredulity on Marlo's face. Marlo states that it doesn't seem possible, and Chris agrees. "That some Spiderman shit right there," Marlo concludes. "We missed our shot. Now he gonna be at us." Neither of the men are overjoyed at the prospect of Omar coming after them, particularly considering his ability to leap from the building and not only survive, but disappear.

Spiderman is the hero of the novel, *Amazing Fantasy*, written in 1770 by

Leland Sirvant and Ditkins Haldwald, the latter also supplying the novel's expressive but anatomically-unlikely illustrations. *Amazing Fantasy* was contemporary to *Man of Tomorrow, Society of Justice*, and other novels of the Gothic tradition, which used the tropes of the knights errant in medieval romances and combined them with darker themes and a heightened, but cartoonish realism. Spiderman himself was a clever hero who defeated evil tyrants and delivered maidens to safety without expectation of reward. Like other Gothic novels, *Amazing Fantasy* featured a setting with extremes of Gothic architecture, including the very tall buildings which Marlo no doubt references.

By invoking Spiderman, Marlo makes Omar into the archetypal hero we have described, and yet the reality is far more mundane. After all this build-up, Ogden finally reveals Omar's actual location: he's in the house itself. While even managing to pull himself into the house is impressive, it's not completely outside the world of possibility, and he has—realistically—sustained significant injury. It's not a superhuman feat, and yet the fact that Omar survived the jump and was not immediately visible afterwards was so dumbfounding, that no one—not even Marlo, who is obviously clever—ever thought to look in the house. Instead, they jump to much more ludicrous conclusions—that Omar was well enough to go home, or to a hospital—that Omar is Spiderman.

Omar is not a mythic hero in *The Wire*. He is mythic hero in Bodymore. Bodymore is meant to be a real city, portrayed with carefully detailed reality. Yet it is within the confines of this realistic setting that myth is born, while the fiction itself—the novel, *The Wire*—is painfully realistic.

In some ways, *The Wire* is about the stories we tell. In the courtroom, "justice" is served by Omar telling lies. Bird has committed murder, even if Omar wasn't there to witness it. In the courtroom excerpt, Ogden demonstrates how the structures of society—in this case, the strictures of the legal system—make it difficult for the truth to be borne out. Meanwhile, in a setting of less structure—a setting of practically social anarchy: the chaos of the street—everyone knows what really happened.

When Omar is eventually killed, in an incident without flourish or romance, by an enemy barely more than a child, no one in the press or government, and few people in the police, care. In the streets, people know the truth. Perhaps paradoxically, it's in the streets that the Omar becomes mythic.

It may be Stringer desired to become legend himself. There is certainly the suggestion that a longing to make a name for himself is part of what motivates Marlo, yet to become "known" in the business world is entirely different than to be known on the streets. Near the end of *The Wire*, Marlo reveals his intentions to renounce his criminal dealings, and like Stringer Bell, become a legitimate industrialist. It is not other industrialists, the business itself, or Marlo's background coming to light that suggest he will not succeed. It is his own longing to construct his identity according to his terms, which is not possible in the real world, no matter how much the ideals of the Victorian Era seems to suggest it could be.

From BOOK V.
Excerpt CHAPTER LX. "—30—."
(March 9, 1852)

The ladies having repaired to the drawing room, Marlo, Mr Levy, and other gentlemen of fine standing enjoyed their brandy and cigars, speaking of manufacturing and trade. Marlo found the conversation dull, though not because he did not highly regard the intricacies of business; he rather was used to leading such discussion, and did not appreciate commerce not his own.

Marlo's attire did not reflect his feelings of incongruity, for indeed his waistcoat was of a finer wool than that of his company, with silver thread embroidering the breast beneath his tailcoat, and the fob which emerged from its pocket was heavy gold. He could not have been distinguished from another gentleman of means and good breeding; he was not among the collarless; and they all called him Mr Stanfield. When a group detached in order to admire the view outside the window casement, however, Marlo did not know of what they spoke; it was gabble composed entirely by men who thought themselves important, and would not remember his name come tomorrow. Furthermore the collar chafed, and Marlo was bored.

These men talked of factories and labour, steam and smoke. These men, these silk and silvered men in collars and in coattails, spoke of building slums, rookeries which would one day rot, factories which would manufacture boots and pins and hunger, workers with brown lungs and families full of sickness. These men spoke of the swelling up of labour, and all the profit to be got from it; they spoke of streets teeming with humanity, factories full of hard work, flats full of bodies.

Marlo was about as good at filling up empty spaces with bones as they were.

There is nothing wrong, of course, in digging graves; it is only filling them that is a crime.

Yet Marlo felt hollowed out somehow, and vacant. Did he, looking down with consternation at the Row, know that men such as he had stood before, looking down upon the world spread out before them—brandy consumed and cigars still smoking—and spoken of dreams? Having achieved the means he had so assiduously applied himself to earn, did Marlo reminisce of days spent upon the streets below him, picking pockets, tricking thieves, and never learning to play croquet? Did he feel that there was nothing more for which to yearn, his aspirations having coalesced into the form of a house for lease, a brougham and silk hat? Or did he feel instead a wistfulness for wealth that could never be achieved—and in that wistfulness, was there betrayal—not of a friend who stood beside him—but of someone he used to be, now that he was once more no one?

"You know who you were talking to?" Mr Levy asked him, after they had all removed to the drawing-room. "He's someone you're gonna wanna know well. But kid, do not get in a room with him alone. You want me in there with you, believe me, or guys like that will bleed you."

Of whomever Mr Levy spoke, he had not known who Marlo was, for Marlo was no Mr Stanfield. Nor did Mr Levy know to whom he spoke, for Marlo could bleed him; indeed, no one in this bright drawing-room, with its tinkling crystal and tapestried walls, was his equal. He could empty them all out, and they would not know why or how, and yet somehow they were not the ones standing in their graves, unknown bodies presiding over unknown houses. He did not know their names, and they did not know his; he already felt bled. To Mr Levy, Marlo was just another body, filling a vacancy in Mr Levy's pocket dug out by Stringer Bell.

Shortly thereafter Marlo managed to extricate himself, claiming only to need a breath of fresh air, but finding once the night closed in around him that he required an escape more complete. Once upon the street, he with some difficulty hailed a hackney cab, for he did not like the idea of calling out his carriage, and the skills of horsemanship were still entirely unknown to him.

It was well past ten-o'-clock when they neared one of the slums over which he had long presided; he told the cab to stop and took his leave, feeling more himself while walking. Hearing boys on the corner talking, he felt still more familiar to himself, knowing that here he belonged; here he was the builder of intention; here he had the connexion that was the foundation to his identity and rooted him to ground.

But the boys were not speaking of trifles, or conquests, or some other foolery with which they had recently been occupied. The boys on the street spoke of Omar, and here Marlo learned the lesson of kings who had come before: the present paid no heed to history, nor to victory. Every age has its heroes; sometimes they are conquerors; more often they are martyrs, and most often they are myth. Myth is by definition make-believe, and yet, because it is remembered it is real in a way that memory did not make Marlo. In three thousand years, will we know better the true streets of Bodymore, their names and the people who walked them, or will we better remember Omar Little? I can tell you the name of Achilles; I cannot tell you the real name of Troy.

"The fuck you looking at?" Marlo demanded of the boy on the street.

"You," said the boy.

"You know who I am?" said Marlo.

"You know who I am?" said the boy, and drew his weapon. Marlo stepped in and drew the boy around, causing the weapon to spin from his hand. The other boy ran as Marlo landed a blow to the first boy's face, and then he was gone too, and Marlo stood alone.

He lifted his arm to see the blood that ran down the elbow of his new tailcoat; he touched it and tasted it, as though to see if it were real. This was not the blood of which Mr Levy had spoken; this was the blood with which Marlo was familiar. This blood was material, was real and warm and flowing.

This was the blood of a body; it bore his name.

CHAPTER V.

FACT AND FICTION.

Man is a pattern seeking, storytelling machine, and the most potent of these stories are those that recur across cultures, across time and regardless of circumstance; the elemental, the mythic. *The Wire* deals not just with myth, but with myth-making itself, which allows Ogden to comment not only on literary tradition, but on the human propensity to expand reality into fiction. Only in the Victorian Age could Romanticism, Gothicism, and poignant satire come to a head in such a trenchant examination of the way archetype endures.

This invention of myth is a significant factor of Book Five, including Marlo's murdered victims, which he stashes in vacant houses, public and official apathy to the killing, and McNulty's crude but effective solution.

In the following excerpt, Marlo's crimes have been discovered, yet the police are unable to provide evidence linking him to the deeds. In the wake of Stringer Bell's downfall, McNulty has receded into the background, preferring to devote himself to family life with the widow Mrs Russel. The discovery of the masses of bodies in the vacant houses, however, causes him to rededicate himself to Scotland Yard.

From BOOK V
Excerpt CHAPTER LII. "Unconfirmed Reports."
(January 13, 1852)

Upon reaching their destination—a large, rambling, half-built structure, more than likely yet another rookery, Mr McNulty and Mr Moreland entered an apartment, led by a police sergeant. This respectable authority explained the events which he believed led to the victim's death, and those circumstances under which he had come to learn of it. No doubt the perpetrator in this instance was an excess of laudanum, for which the victim himself could be blamed; there did not appear to be anyone connected to the poor fellow who might have wished him ill or well.

Mr Moreland inquired as to whether the necessary artists and physicians had had an opportunity to survey the scene, whereupon the sergeant replied that the wait was two or three hours. Mr Moreland sighed, unsurprised. "Shit gets worse every day."

Mr McNulty, meanwhile, was examining the body, hearing this conversation between the sergeant and Mr Moreland as a sort of background, similar to the songs of washerwomen of an evening, or the clop of horse hooves on the street. These were every day sounds: the slow inefficiency of Scotland Yard, the unconcern and helplessness of anyone involved—even Mr Moreland, and the pointlessness of the dead man spread out before Mr McNulty. Here they wasted time and resources of two detectives, artists and a doctor, this policeman and who knew what else. No one cared for this poor fellow; his case would only be solved because it could be with relative ease, whereas the case of Marlo Stanfield's vacant houses would not be merely due to the miniscule matter of a dearth of capital. Two or three hours and "shit" getting worse every day were sounds McNulty felt that he heard all the time; they were the sounds of a pump flowing with a steady, "drip, drip, drip," and long intervals between: the intermittent monotone was the noise of no one caring. Mr McNulty was becoming exhausted by the sound of nothing. He longed to make the pump flow.

"Jimmy," Mr Moreland said suddenly, breaking into his reverie. Mr McNulty raised his brows, glancing at his partner. "You okay?" Mr Moreland asked.

There was no way to make the dead man before him into a clergyman's daughter lost in Aruba, though Mr McNulty supposed that this victim, as one alone and helpless, might at least garner more attention than Marlo's victims, were there only several dozen more of them.[1] It occurred to Mr McNulty then that there were several dozen more of just such men; excepting the fact that they all died under different circumstances, they might as well have been the men in Marlo's vacants. Just then, within the churning miasma of Mr McNulty's mind, a small tendril of thought began to form, a scheme dastardly and daring—arising from that conversation at the public-house the night before, but called up also from places even darker, deep within.

We define numbers and rates as reality: the definite measure of worldly

---

[1] This is a reference to a scene not included, in which McNulty, Bunk, and Freamon discuss the "ideal" victim they assume will garner media and public attention. The victim they concot is a clergyman's daughter visiting the West Indies. Although obscure today, her visiting Aruba would have clued the Victorian reader into the social standing of such a woman, without directly referencing her class or wealth.

experience, palpable and cold. The truth, however, cannot be told with figures any more than it can be with faeries, for the truth is fuller than any figure which could support it; there is no arithmetic that quantifies the wealth of human experience. Yet as soon as we would speak to that experience, we embellish it, for experience itself does not exist but in perception, and all perception is but fantasy. We therefore are suspended forever in purgatory between fact and fiction; the story of the truth holds less meaning the more it is sprinkled with numeric values and percentages, and less credibility when elaborated upon with make-believe. Were I to tell you the story of Mr McNulty's continued careful courtship of Mrs Russell, reader, would you believe it? And were I to continue to list instance after instance of his impotent action, wherein he never moves beyond an equilibrium of frustration and resigned acceptance, his sanity perfectly intact—would you continue to turn the page? Please forgive this Author for refusing you, dear reader, the opportunity of finding out.

The figures that serve to obscure the truth in this account are myriad, but those which in particular consumed the mind of Mr McNulty were those facts against which Bunny Colvin so disreputably rallied—that of the criminal statistics. Mr Colvin, with his experiment in Hamsterdam, had demonstrated most effectively that numbers did not tell the whole story, for while theft, murder, and any number of other types of crime had effectively dropped, Hamsterdam remained fact. That particular assay having ended, the avenue left open in Mr McNulty's mind lay in the opposite direction: that of sensational fiction. People clung to fantasy as stubbornly as to figures. This was what he, Mr Moreland, and Mr Freamon had been discussing the night previous: the clergyman's daughter lost in the West Indies had all the trappings of a fable. From it could be spun elaborate yarns of grief and despair; Ceres might weep for Proserpina and winter might fall. Spring would come with her return and the six seeds she had consumed within the bowels of the earth, for the history of humanity demonstrated a tendency to explain fact with fiction.

Mr McNulty now contemplated the idea of telling truth by parable. He wondered whether there were any other way that reality could be recognized.

Standing up, he gestured to the sergeant. "Go get a coffee," he advised, explaining that the policeman was no doubt needed back on the street, and that he and his colleague had the situation well in hand. Glancing at Mr

Moreland, he further expounded, "We've got to wait on him anyway." He turned back to the sergeant. "Go ahead."

The policeman, surprised, thanked him and returned to his duty.

"Don't let this guy go anywhere," Mr McNulty advised Mr Moreland, walking away from the corpse. He gave an awkward cough, explaining that he was going to fetch some piece of equipment, to which Mr Moreland said, "Bring the paper in, will you?" Mr McNulty paused, considering the penny dreadful he was about to concoct, while Mr Moreland explained, "We're going to be here a while."

When Mr McNulty returned, he had fortified himself with rye whiskey. Mr Moreland was already smoking a cigar, which he removed upon seeing his associate. His eyes went to the bottle peeking out of Mr McNulty's frock coat, saying, "Little early for that, ain't it?"

Mr McNulty ignored him, and went for the body. His knocking over a chair and bucket beside it provoked Mr Moreland to remove his cigar a second time. "What the fuck are you doing?" he queried, in tones of incredulity.

"Just watch the door, Bunk," Mr McNulty advised, stepping over the body.

"Shit." Mr Moreland scowled, but he had been in the habit of working with Mr McNulty for years, through which he had gained an instinct to help his friend and at times, follow his lead. He glanced to the doorway. No one was there, which apparently incited Mr McNulty to begin throwing himself at the walls.

These structures were not unassailable, the timber lacking reinforcement in several places, such that Mr McNulty's banging could bring about extreme damage. While Mr Moreland had no care for the house, he still had some small concern for a crime scene, and moreover a regard for his partner. They had drawn up entire series of events merely by looking at small holes and angles through windows; together, they could inference conclusions upon evidence in sketches and measurements made with tape. While such meticulous investigation often annoyed him, Mr Moreland took a certain pride in it. Many people, considering his size and bluff manner, might consider him an indelicate man; neither they nor most people possessed the powers of observation of intricate insight he and Mr McNulty employed when faced with sensitive details.

This was understood between them almost equivocally, for while Mr McNulty frequently boasted of his accomplishments, Mr Moreland preferred not to think of them at all. Indeed, in similar circumstances at different times, he and Mr McNulty had conducted their investigations without more than a word or two spoken between them, intrinsically understanding the minutia which built together into human action.

Now Mr McNulty defaced said minutia, not to mention an entire wall, for no reason that Mr Moreland could discern. "Whoa," he said, "come on, Jimmy." He gave another nervous glance toward the door. "Get a fucking grip."

Mr McNulty appeared to assess his damage to the wall, but not in response to the remonstrance of Mr Moreland, who had re-inserted his cigar and was chomping vigorously in consternation. Instead, Mr McNulty moved from the wall, and straight-away fell upon the corpse, rubbing some bit of loose mortar from the wall upon the victim's worsted trousers.

"Jimmy!" Mr Moreland protested, in some shock, but still Mr McNulty did not heed him. Instead, he moved directly to the victim's shoulder, tearing the cloth of that pitiful man's coat. "You lost your fucking mind?"

Pushing the corpse from him, Mr McNulty knelt, as though appraising his recent frantic work. Quickly, he made the sign of the cross over his chest in recognition of that Roman religion to which his forebears ascribed.

Martyrs were not martyrs until myths were made.

He stood again over the corpse. Reaching down, he placed his hands around the throat of the deceased victim, adjusting his hands in a kind of caress. Then, with a grunt, he began to choke the dead body.

Mr Moreland ejaculated an oath, calling the name of a man who lived in memory for his murder. "You sick fuck," he added, disgust coursing in his tone. With a groan, he moved away, unable to watch, as though perhaps behind him there occurred not only the desecration of the dead victim, but of his friend as well.

When he returned, Mr McNulty had straightened, his expression wiped clean and replaced with that incorrigible smile of which so many authorities had despaired. Nodding to the corpse, he thereupon proffered an explanation: someone had killed this man; he had died because he was weak, alone, and friendless. The killer needed to be caught, Mr McNulty cautioned. He took a large swig of the whiskey from his bottle and grinned, a macabre gesture of camaraderie.

Mr Moreland looked from him to the corpse, disgust still etched heavily in his features. Holding up his hands, he said, "I'm gone." For while Mr Moreland had previously assisted Mr McNulty in dishonest schemes, and had himself at time circumvented the law in the name of justice, this atrocity before him was not just. This was criminal, and while Mr Moreland would not inform on his friend, nor would he be a party to desecration. Having told Mr McNulty so, Mr Moreland made good his exit.

Mr McNulty, seeming unperturbed by this departure, continued his charade by rolling the corpse, and grasping by the dead fellow's belt in order to pull him into a folded position. He rubbed down the jacket of the poor man, and then found himself patting the victim's back in precisely the way he might have pounded Bunk Moreland's, for now the dead chap was his only partner in this venture. Mr McNulty knew his actions to be objectionable on every front which Mr Moreland might protest, but Mr McNulty planned to continue them, even into searching for the dead man's killer.

Standing back from the corpse again, Mr McNulty quaffed another draught of whiskey rye, that fortifying liquid without which he might not have had the courage to perform murder on a man who was already dead.

* * *

It would be difficult to find a character in Victorian literature comparable to the deeply charming, richly flawed James "Jimmy" McNulty. While McNulty is rich in his own right, he is particularly interesting in comparison to the viewpoint characters of Dickens. As Dickens progressed from his "picaresque" adventure-style novels to his more serious explorations of society, so too did his central protagonist evolve. And yet, instead of gaining in complexity, Dickens' viewpoint characters dwindled—in personality, idiosyncrasy, any unique or identifying traits.

Some scholars believe the passivity of Dickens' heroes was a direct result of his shift in style and subject matter: in order to portray the many aspects of society Dickens wished to explore, in order to maintain a strong supporting cast of highly individualized characters, the main character must be de-individualized. He must become a receptacle of the injustices perpetrated by society, so that the failure of social institution can be witnessed and explored as the reader identifies with the protagonist's essential powerlessness. This is an elegant method, used to near-perfection in *David Copperfield*, in which the only uninteresting character is David Copperfield himself.

The Wire charted another course. McNulty is a challenging character: vulgar, skilled, admirable at times, and reprehensible at others. Though he is our protagonist and usually our viewpoint character on our journey through *The Wire*, he begins and ends on notes that are extremely morally questionable, despite a redemptive arc mid-series. We are unable to approve of his actions, unable to assimilate his qualities as our own. Yet McNulty is powerless exactly in the way of David Copperfield or Pip from *Great Expectations*, used and exploited by corrupt social systems, institutions, or figures of power. He is helpless to incite real and lasting change, his passivity forced on him by the world rather than arising from a lack of internal agency. It is this very struggle which endears McNulty to us, in the end.

It is this, too, which causes McNulty to invent the false killer. As McNulty, Bunk, and Freamon discuss in the tavern, those that know about Marlo and the dozens of dead bodies found in the slums don't seem to care. This apathy, however, was not about heartlessness, but about weariness, and a lack of specificity. They could come to care if the story were new. The murder of the homeless is fresh and sensational: it gives people an individual narrative to latch on to in the morass of social injustice which leads to constant crime and death.

In a sense, Marlo's victims mattered less because they were part of a much bigger—and ultimately unsolvable—problem. Industrialization, as has been seen, resulted not only in the growth of the bourgeoisie and working class, but in the growth of poverty and homelessness in urban settings. However, the population of the poor was so immense, the crimes and tragedies so frequent and numerous, that the problem could not be taken on one person at a time. It became possible to see people not as individuals, but as masses. The Victorian Era marked the rise of the nameless, faceless poor, who could not be dealt with individually, only numerically.

The importance and nature of numbers and statistics play a large part in *The Wire*. Scotland Yard is concerned with the number of annual crimes. The unions are concerned with the number of jobs. Carcetti is concerned with his number of votes. The newspapers are concerned with their number of readers, and all of these people, systems, and institutions rely on the ultimate number: amount of money.

Marlo's victims are among those nameless, faceless numbers. Poverty, as an inevitable outcome of progress, could not be helped. Even more detrimentally, there were those who assumed that the poor could take advantage of the opportunities offered by the Industrial Revolution, if they were clever or hard-working enough. The conclusion is natural: crimes in the slums were solely a result of the "quality" of people who inhabited them, and had nothing to do with the social institutions which resulted in slums in the first place. The public, unable to eliminate the problems caused by poverty, and feeling it hopeless to assist people on a case by case basis, became inured to the horrors occurring amongst the "rabble."

However, the invented victim in Aruba would not have belonged to the rabble. She would have had a name and a face, which is why McNulty, Bunk, and Freamon dream that such a scenario would catch the public's attention.

This is another case of myth or fantastic fiction—in this case, horror—being created not only in spite of, but because of realistic circumstances. That the public is uninterested in Marlo or Marlo's crimes is realistic. That McNulty is disappointed in this and seeking a way to circumvent the limitations of said disinterest creates is realistic. The solution McNulty creates—his killer—is unrealistic, but is it unrealistic that McNulty invents it? What other way was there to get the public's attention, and thus get the money and personnel needed to combat Marlo's group?

Just before Marlo is arrested, Deputy Daniels—McNulty and Freamon's boss—meets with Steintorf, right-hand man to Carcetti. Steintorf tells the police they need to bring down crime in the city, in order to burnish Carcetti's reputation. Daniels patiently explains the steps neccessary to take down Marlo, but Steintorf doesn't seem to particularly care. What he cares about are the numbers. "Be creative," he advises Daniels.

Directly after Daniels' conversation with Steintorf, Freamon informs him that they can arrest Marlo. The arrest of Marlo is a compelling, satisfying scene, a rare moment of readerly gratification: after looming up over the world of Bodymore for the past two volumes of *The Wire*, at last we see Marlo Stanfield on his knees. And yet, the victory does not last. McNulty's lie is revealed, and so Marlo is unable to be prosecuted.

The Wire makes the case that society has two ways of dealing with its massive urban population: one is statistics, and the other is sensationalism, and neither one is precisely truth. McNulty's killer is a fiction, but so too are the crime statistics. The latter may be accurate, and yet they do not tell the whole story. The story, however, can only be told through the lens of human perception, and it is that lens that leads to fantastic story-telling, and the very myth-making which

The Wire explores. The story of Marlo Stanfield lies somewhere in between Steintorf's crime rates and McNulty's killer, and yet, because of the time and care it takes to tell it, it is a truth untold in Bodymore.

It would be easy to repudiate the plot of Book Five, to claim that Ogden, for some reason, abandoned his dedication to the semblance of reality which seems to be *The Wire*'s goal. It would be easy to suspect that *The Wire* falls prey to the very behavior it condemns, by providing us with a sensational plot—a plot which is in essence about the creation of a sensational plot.

Yet *The Wire* cannot help but become in some sense mythic, taking on the very narrative framework that the novel shows is most likely to garner understanding and response from the general public. Even though Omar is portrayed realistically, he becomes mythic in the readers' minds because in the realistic setting of *The Wire*, real characters see him as mythic. And even though *The Wire* comments on our propensity towards sensationalism, it itself becomes sensational.

The Wire could have been a list. It could have been a ledger sheet, criminal statistics all in a row, or a precise enumeration of those many lives lived and ended in poverty. Conversely, it could be all action and sentiment and spectacle, a penny dreadful, instead of educating serving only to titillate. Instead, Ogden gave us a story, and though it is framed by narrative and fiction, it is grasping for the truth.

Ogden never sugarcoats. There are no happy endings. Even if he doesn't give us exact reality, nor does he give us epic struggles or the ultimate triumph of good over evil. Although there is myth in *The Wire*, the story that is told is unrelentingly human.

The following excerpt depicts one such human in a rare moment of lightness and subtle triumph.

From BOOK V.
Excerpt CHAPTER LV. "React Quotes."
(February 3, 1852)

The cook-shop in Mount Street is kept by an old Papist whom everyone calls Viva; if one should chance by this shop most days of the year, one would conclude from the size of the crowds that the pudding was highly to be admired. Upon stepping in, one would receive the information that the fare comes at no cost, and one is invited to sit at the board and partake of said offerings, exactly as though one were an old friend. By now one has grown suspicious, suspecting the provisions may prove paltry or full of worms; one looks about at one's fellow meal-goers and begins to suspect that they are vagrants, criminals, and ticket-of-leave men. Indeed, one looks out the window, and upon such collection of evidence, notices that many of those crowded around are children with thin faces; one begins to understand he is in a different sort of cook-shop than he at first supposed. But then the meal is served, and it is piping hot; the stew steams with meat, and scraps of bread prove hearty when dipped in the broth. One finds one's company is of a varied degree, from the ticket-of-leave men earlier suspected, to those having become recently unemployed due to inclement weather, to those poor factory souls—who, having employment, still find themselves unable to feed their families.

It is in this Viva House on Mount Street, not two or three years ago, one might also have found a lanky fellow of otherwise good proportion. This fellow, though lacking in formal address or studied manner, would prove himself to be engaging both in disposition and conversation, and despite his neat apron and collarless state, one would have found him peculiarly knowledgeable on the subject of silk and velvet hats. This gentleman—so he is, and so we shall call him, though others may beg to differ—began by washing iron and copper pots by the pump directly behind the establishment. So honest was his labour, and so agreeable his general deportment, that the Italian—a fine, discerning gentleman—invited him forward, where he was admitted to the kitchen. If one were to try the pudding—which, the reader will recall, was one's original intent upon entering the establishment—one would not only discover it to indeed be admirable; one would find it to be ladled up by that very same gentleman who began by scrubbing pots.

If one had been at all acquainted with the fellow by means of this account or some others' (this Author is not so proud as to suggest that his is the only record of this gentleman's previous adventures; indeed, as you will see, Michael Fletcher has written his own article, which can no doubt be found in the periodical published at about the date of this reporting), one would be hard pressed to recognize him at Viva House, for he was much changed. Not only had this gentleman renounced his occupation as a pedlar and his career as an addict; he had settled down nicely in the cellar of his sister's abode, and his

face had mostly cleared. Where one was used to witness the redness about the eyes and various lesions that speak to that sickness of soul which he was once unable to cure; one would now have found a clear face and healthy smile. Were one graced with the opportunity to search within the heart of that man, one might not have discovered it to be completely healed, for such miracles are worked only with time. Memories of his friend Sherrod, his own weakness and his feeling of betrayal, sometimes crowded in upon our poor, friendly fellow, until it seemed to him useless to continue his constant toil of lugging boiling kettles, and pouring tea. Still, he persevered.

Scott Templeton once stopped by Mount Street in his quest to describe the plight of the homeless and destitute, but he found there nothing to interest him. The mere histories of survival held no fascination for our headlines, which long only for sensation. Yet Michael Fletcher, stopping here, encountered that very gentleman whom I have mentioned, and heard from him a story so human that he stayed a while, and listened.

We know and love the stories in which nobility and honour prevail, and sin is demolished. We even have found some interest in tales in which greed gains a foothold, only to be destroyed ultimately by some powerful and vital force. But the very best stories are not of Evil laid to waste; they are not of corruption that ceases to exist; they are not of pestilence which at last grows cold, sparse, and dies. The very best Book, though twisted and perverted, bent to the use of those who would gain power and misuse it, is not the tale of Good defeating Evil, for Evil has never been destroyed. It walks among us, and the only thing to be done against it is to keep a constant vigilance. The only thing to be done is to push it back where it belongs, underground, in its hole.

The story of Bubbles, dear reader, is not that of a man which rises from this bleak Earth unto Heaven. It is the story of a man who ascends from the cellar to the parlour, where there is a dinner of mutton and greens to be enjoyed with his sister, who has forgiven him.

* * *

The Wire's deepest deviation from other Victorian novels comes in its bleak moral outlook. Even Dickens' darkest works have a handful of characters that are essentially likeable. In the end, the power of love and truth is borne out and the individual triumphs over the ugliness of society by maintaining his integrity. Trollope, Eliot, Gaskell, etc. all write with this essentially Western—not to mention imperialist—mind-set. Only William Makepeace Thackeray's *Vanity Fair*—subtitled, *A Novel Without A Hero*—presents a truly bleak assessment of society. The ending is unhappy, all of the characters flawed to varying degrees. It is significant that critics of the time chastised Thackeray for refusing to throw his audience crumbs of moral fiber.

The other comparison one might draw in examining the moral character of *The Wire* is the penny dreadful: Victorian booklets which exploited sensationalist drama, horror, and Gothic tradition. Penny dreadfuls were fiction published on pulp and could be purchased for a penny per pamphlet, and often featured monsters, vampires, highwaymen, and crooks. Usually, these publications bear little similarity to the highbrow syndications of the time, their cliché down to an art form, their treatment of hackney topics procedural in nature.

By 1846, the time *The Wire* first began syndication, the Victorian audience was already familiar with an underworld of crime, the systems arrayed against it, the cops-and-robbers story. But while only the penny dreadful exceeds *The Wire* in its depictions of violence, ugliness, and depravity of the world, these procedurals should be considered as a separate genre. They reached for the simple thrills of titillation. Meanwhile, *The Wire* had pretenses of social commentary, exposing deeper truths, persuading its readers not only to witness the details of a corrupt society, but also to understand it.

Morality in Art was one of the most prevailing topics in both literary criticism and philosophy of Victorian times, propounded by art critic and philosopher John Ruskin. Ruskin's central argument was that one must reveal Truth in literature, but in doing so also reveal Beauty. One must present the moral beacon to which we all must aspire. One must not write without Hope. It is significant also that today, Thackeray is not charged with undue cynicism or depravity; rather, he is thought to be sentimental.

Literature today is no longer concerned with morality the way it was in the nineteenth century. Unrelenting, bleak images of society are celebrated for their realism, as representations of humanity. And yet, we have very few images, representations, or new and challenging canon that captures the essential helplessness, the inevitable corruption, the deep-lying flaws of both society and humanity in the manner of *The Wire*.

The counterpoint to Bubbles' quiet triumph is Duquan. Duquan is a poor, homeless boy who has shown both amiability and aptitude for learning in Pryzbylewski's class. However, like some of the other students, he suffers in the school system, which pays more attention to test scores than individual students. Though Pryzbylewski takes a special interest in him, he is unable to devote the time an energy to fully protect Duquan from circumstances, and Duquan himself is ultimately unable to rise above them.

From BOOK V
Excerpt CHAPTER X. "—30—."
(March 9, 1852)

"Hey," said Dukie, by way of greeting.

"Duquan," said Mr Pryzbylewski. "Hello."

Just then, a pupil passed by a tight group of children in the yard who were enjoying the small bit of food they had brought in pails from home. The pupil in question knocked down a bit of bread held by another boy, whereby Mr Pryzbylewski immediately interceded, quelling the possibility of altercation, and threatening the child with further detention. Dukie observed all this with a slow smile, for although he had no desire to remember all that Mr P had hoped on his account, he did recall the early days of Mr P's tutorship at Tilghman. In those days, Mr P had needed the assistance of Mrs Sampson merely to control his own students; he never would have been able to corral such discipline in the yard, where the students behaved more freely, thinking themselves beyond supervision. Dukie thought that whatever happened this afternoon, Mr P was now enjoying a measure of success. He could not be too disappointed.

"Looks like you got the hang of it," Dukie said, still smiling, as the reprimanded student reentered the schoolhouse wearing a hangdog expression, and Mr P turned in his direction.

Mr P only nodded. "What's up with you, Duquan?"

Dukie stood. "Oh, it ain't nothing."

Mr P asked after his boarding school, to which Dukie replied with a shrug, explaining that he and the other boys had been released for a visit home, though of course this was a falsehood. He did not mind, however, Mr P understanding the difficulty of such leave-taking, explaining, "I'm outdoors now." This he punctuated with little movements of his hand, such that his old teacher might understand what he meant by "outdoors," for Mr P had been quite a good deal more aware than some of his particular circumstances, and had been a good deal more given to generosity as well. This generosity was, of course, the reason Dukie had come.

Seeing that Mr P understood, Dukie went on, "I was hoping, maybe I could visit you, borrow some money, so I can get a place and some clean clothes and get myself settled, so then I could go back to school."

"You're on the street?" said Mr Pryzbylewski.

Dukie clasped his hands. "I mean, I got some people ready to gimme a really really good place if I come up with some money for it." Then he let his hands drop, closed his mouth, and looked at Mr Pryzbylewski, who had always believed in him. Dukie knew he should feel ashamed. Instead, he felt not a thing.

Mr Pryzbylewski was quiet for a long time. When he spoke, it was with that same gentle tone which he had used countless times—a tone that held no censure, nor any condemnation. Dukie had too great an intelligence to suppose that Mr Pryzbylewski had none; Mr P knew what he was asking. "How much do you need?" was the question.

Steeling himself, Dukie named the amount. "But, if you're willing to go one-fifty more, I can enroll in the G.E.D. program down at B.C.C.C.[1]

---

[1] **one-fifty more:** this might refer to as little as a shilling and sixpence, considering Duquan's circumstances, but taking into account the comment by the arabber that ends the scene, one-fifty is probably slang for a much greater sum. The amount probably refers to a sovereign and crown; **G.E.D:** Duquan is most likely referring to an apprenticeship. Before the Industrial Revolution, the most common education of the middle class was through the guild system, in which a young man might apprentice himself to a craftsman or shopkeeper. By working with a master, a man might earn the position of a journeyman, eventually mastering the craft and taking on his own business, or running the shop after the master's death. Duquan most likely volunteered this information because he knew Mr Pryzbylewski wanted him to receive an education, which he would not have been able to had he supplied a different lie, such as working in a factory. Although Duquan's lie is plausible, it seems unlikely, and Mr Pryzbylewski no doubt knows it: it would have been difficult for a member of the lower class such as Duquan to serve even as apprentice. It required more initial capital than he is asking, and he wouldn't have the time or skills necessary to even be taken on by a master. Furthermore, the guild system was fading out of practice by the time *The Wire* was published, though there were still experts in various fields which specialized in handmade goods, even as there are today (Freamon is an example of such a master).

Then I can get my G.E.D. without having to go back to Southwestern, and I can get my work permit."[2]

Mr P did not appear as amenable as a man might, upon learning that the hopes he had bestowed upon a child might come to fruition so shortly in such a tidy manner. Instead, he looked disappointed. His voice, however, did not change timbre. He was still very steady and warm when he proposed to hire a cab to drive Dukie to this shop, so that Mr Pryzbylewski might arrange things with the draper, and see that Duquan was indeed to be taken on as an assistant.

"No, Mr P, you ain't got to do all that," said Dukie, looking somewhat shifty. Bethinking himself an expedient, he added quickly, "Besides, I really ain't got the time to go down there today. But, you know, I'm gonna."

Mr Pryzbylewski was quiet for another little while. "I can do it, Duquan, if that's what you want, and I don't even care about the money. But understand, I'm gonna go down to B.C.C.C. in a few days, and find out if you're enrolled. And if you are, then I can say, 'Great! Duquan can come past with his certificate when he gets it, and we're still friends. He can still rely on me.' But if you aren't enrolled . . . well. I imagine I'm not gonna see you again, am I?"

Dukie had smiled his unruly, winning smile, and had called him 'Mr P' for the last time, reassuring him that all would be well.

Mr Pryzbylewski smiled as well, a weak, sickly thing. He still did not say he did not trust him. Instead, he explained that he would get his things and meet Dukie on the street so that they might hire a cab.

Duquan nodded and looked down. Mr Pryzbylewski left, and the other children laughed and passed him in the school yard.

Once in possession of the draft from the bank, Mr Pryzbylewski and Duquan travelled in the hackney cab to a part of town with which Mr Pryzbylewski was at least moderately familiar, having spent evenings patrolling this very area. It was on the edge of a slum, and Dukie

---

[2] A "G.E.D." was most likely the equivalent of journeyman status. "B.C.C.C." is the name of a draper's shop, the initials probably comprising the names of the masters (and proprietors) to whom Duquan might apprentice. "Southwestern" refers to the boarding school from which he has escaped. "Work permit" is similar to a certificate of mastery; if neither B nor C nor C nor C died within a given period of time, instead of waiting to inherit, Duquan might take on his own business. Again, this seems unlikely, as Duquan is not in the position to move through the ranks in this way.

directed them deeper to the mouth of a street with tall narrow buildings on either side. Mr Pryzbylewski could not see into the shadows
of the alley, despite the sunlight earnestly shining on the cobbles of the street,
growing more feeble as it approached the alley's depths.

Mr Pryzbylewski could not help reflecting on his own words as
Dukie opened climbed out of the cab. Here he was in his linen suit, not well-
tailored but at least smart and presentable in the manner of a school teacher,
and here was Dukie, wearing the lines not of pressed linen on his body, nor in
his attitude the lines of arithmetic which Mr Pryzbyleski had forced him to
draw out on his slate, but under his eyes lines of age, as though he had already
lived a thousand years since Mr Pryzbylewski had last seen him.

"We can still be friends," Mr Pryzbylewski had told him.

Now as Mr Pryzbylewski watched Dukie walk down into the alley, he ex-
amined the results of his conditions, for he felt sure as to the state of Duquan's
enrollment at the B.C.C. Now Dukie could not rely on him, and they were
not friends. Mr Pryzbylewski would have liked to remain friends; in his heart
of hearts, this street urchin for whom he had come to care so dearly would
always be someone of whom he thought affectionately, someone to whom his
bosom clung with thoughts of hope though there was none, someone whose
spirit—cheerful, clever, and unflagging—was pure and innocent. For a fleeting
moment, Mr Pryzbylewski wished that spirit had already flown this wretched
body, had shaken off the shackles of the morbid state of mortality; he wished
that the poor body trudging to meet the figure in the alley was only an empty shell, rightfully seeking its destruction in order that it may join its lighter,
cleaner counterpart.

But Mr Pryzbylewski knew better than that. The soul could not escape
its body any more than Duquan could escape the life opening up before him.
Only Mr Pryzbylewski could drive away, which he did, when the arabber asked
Dukie, "How much?" and Dukie looked back to make sure Mr P had gone
from this world that he could poke and prod, but never, in essence, change.

"Two hundred," said Dukie.[3]

"Damn, boy," said the arabber. "Teacher must love your black ass."

Dukie looked back in the direction Mr Pryzbylewski had driven the gig,

---

[3] Most likely two pounds. Again, judging by the arabber's reaction, it could even be a tenner.

certain that Mr P had known that he was not enrolled, and that the money he had lent him would be used for purposes of which Mr P would not approve. And yet, Mr P had still given him the money. The arabber was right of course: Mr P did love him.

But love could not help you escape: love was sitting in Mr Pryzbyleski's gig, which would always drive away in the end, because love could not be injected into veins, where it would stay and keep you warm, holding you close until you fell asleep, and tender freedom came at last in the form of dreams of kind words, warm summer days spent with friends, and Michael.

CHAPTER VI.

AFTERLIFE.

A hundred and fifty years from now, what works of our culture will remain? Pokémon coloring books, a *Friends* DVD box set, a box full of Terry Pratchett novels. The popular survives, and so, by the time of Ogden's death, *The Wire*'s chances did not look good. During its initial serialization, it was largely ignored, some scholars and critics taking notice, but much of the public indifferent to its charms. This was occasionally reflected in the press, but is most evident in personal letters or off-hand references:

Letter from Thomas Carlyle, dated February 8, 1848

[. . .] While out walking the other night (Thursday last), I thought I spotted Charles Dickens. Aware that the poor man must be mobbed at any opportunity good fortune so accords, I turned toward him. He was not Charles. He did not look a bit like Charles. In fact, so disappointingly unlike Charles was he, I am hard pressed to discover why I mistook him for Charles, or indeed, why anyone might do so. There before me was a rough brute of a fellow, and our friend Charles is sweetly disposed, gentle and kind! Oh, that man before me was as well-formed, as they all say, but that is the best that can be said for him; for although he is talented and clever, he makes the whole world out to be wretched. First he bores us frightfully until we are almost forced to give up his company entirely, and then he makes us tear out our hair; he makes us shake our fists; he makes us weep. Charles—though he may cause a tear or two to escape the confines of our eyes—would never have the ill-natured disregard to abandon us in such a state. Charles, seeing our pathetic condition, would have a little mercy; Charles, seeing we are cold, would throw a coat about our shivering shoulders; seeing that we cry, he would offer us his own hand kerchief. By Charles we are cheered considerably; soon we are jolly again, and begin to enjoy ourselves. This is the nature of friendship!—that we should be tossed about from time to time, but in the end we should make amends; friendship is for a ride in the park on a sunny day, and for taking tea together at noon-time—as well as for the purpose of shoring up our souls.

But there before me on the Embankment was a man who dislikes everybody, a man who is kind to no-one, a man who makes us disappointed in our fellows, and champions not a single one of our acquaintance, though some are in appearances quite good. "You are not Charles Dickens!" I exclaimed to this man, and thereupon I turned about on a heel and left, for though I have been told most often that once I am used to his ugly demeanour and crude manners, I shall grow to like him; I have yet to understand why I should bother—if he is not, after all, Charles Dickens![. . .]

The letter suggests that Ogden was fairly well-known at the time, or at least talked about, even if Carlyle initially "mistook" him for Dickens. The implication is that Ogden came highly recommended, and yet no one wanted to actually take the time to slog through the five volume masterpiece. Indeed, we have even found a reference or two citing *The Wire* as "the best novel ever written," and yet the public's reaction remained cool.

Still, not all of his contemporaries scorned Ogden. In fact, though most of *The Wire*'s sincere followers appear to be among the unknown masses, a great admirer of his work is widely known today: Charlotte Brontë.

As this London Standard editorial cartoon suggests, even if *The Wire* was not a runaway success comparable to *Great Expectations*, Ogden and his ideas were getting some attention, although that attention could be far from favorable.

Charlotte Brontë (as Currer Bell) to H.B. Ogden, January 17, 1849

Sir,

I am writing in response to a little review of The Wire which appeared recently in the Review—no doubt you have seen the one to which I refer—I have no doubt furthermore that though I know naught of you but that which has been published, which remains for the most part in fictional form—that we are in accord in regards to this review—that, in short, we are charmed by its smallness. The aspersions cast upon your work The Wire are most quaint—I cannot help but feel they must have been made by a little person knowing little of the world, while at times I think you must be familiar with all of history—that of man, but also those small, irrelevant histories: that of the doctor in Harley Street, that of the curate on the moor, that of a small, unknown young man from Yorkshire who has written some small trifle—these little oddities I feel at times you must know, so genuinely do you detail your own histories. While I cannot claim one fraction of the vast experience so obviously at your disposal, I must admit to feeling that the shadows cast upon Wuthering Heights are of a similar shape—similarly small, and similarly ignorant.

Wuthering Heights is small in scope in comparison to your vast undertaking, but I think our little reviewer was not untoward in his comparison—if you will pardon my presumption; as you may guess from my surname, I am related to the author of that work, though Ellis has recently passed from this mortal coil—while I remain behind, and his work, I hope, immortal.

I do not write, however, to draw the comparisons that the delightful fellow who wrote that little critique espouses—but rather to state that I am following The Wire, even if our charming colleague is not. I think it a work of the highest calibre—I admire the unflinching way in which you portray its characters, who suffer under the burden of a most oppressive tyranny—that of continued injustice and constant usury, and the way some characters shine like some unpolished copper or brass amongst midden, under all this weight—and the way some become unrepentant demons. In particular I admire Omar—whose courage, I think, would be deemed fanciful and mere romance, were he penned by a woman—but under a masculine surname the pen always produces a masculine portrait, be he ever so driven by love, and the finer concerns of the heart.

Ardently awaiting the next instalment of The Wire,
I remain yours most respectfully,
Currer Bell

The review she mentions appears in the *Westminster Review* in January, 1849:

> [. . .] We are not following H.B. Ogden's *The Wire* [. . .] We find ourselves revolted by its morbid insistence on wallowing in darkness, among characters we despise, and issues which do not interest the God-fearing, moral man. In such a narrative as Ogden has construct-ed, one would think to find at least one man, pure and unblackened, working on the side of justice. But indeed, after minimal perusal, we find no such man. The so-called heroes of this work are like that of another work published the year previous, which appeared in the wake of its greater, sister work, with barely a ripple to mark its presence, and deservedly so. And though *The Wire* and *Wuthering Heights* differ so much in particulars, they mirror each other's perversity beyond the extent of their characters and subject matter, for both employ a mys-tifying, esoteric style. Indeed, the slow build of *The Wire*, the gradual heaping-on of more and more plots and characters, the amorphous structure in which society's ills, rather than individuals, seem to be the central theme, reminds us of *Wuthering Heights* framework of a story told within a story within a story—a oppugnant construction which leaves the reader far outside the central narrative [. . .]

This searing criticism appeared in the *Review* a full year after *Wuthering Heights* had been published, but no doubt would have struck Charlotte par-ticularly hard. Emily—her sister and *Heights'* author—died the month before the review appeared. The sisters were close, and it is understandable that Char-lotte would have been defensive of Emily's work. Some of her comments about Heathcliffe, the hero of *Heights*, could easily be transposed onto someone like Avon Barksdale, or even Marlo Stanfield: "[Heathcliff] exemplifies the effects which a life of continued injustice and hard usage may produce [. . .]. Carefully trained and kindly treated, the black gipsy-cub might possibly have been reared into a human being [. . .]." (Charlotte to William Smith Williams, August 14, 1848)

The Wire and *Wuthering Heights* are such vastly different works that it's not surprising there appear to be no other criticisms linking them. However, the reception of *Heights*, and even the reviews of the other Brontë novels, do bear a distinct similarity in some ways to those of *The Wire*. It is understandable that Charlotte would draw connections between herself and Ogden and Ogden and her sister. A review of *Wuthering Heights* and *Agnes Gray* (by Anne Brontë, publishing under the pen names Ellis and Acton Bell, respectively) from the *Athenaeum* on Christmas day, 1847, states:

> The Bells seem to affect painful and exceptional subjects—the misdeed and oppressions of tyranny [. . .] They do not turn away from dwelling on those physical acts of cruelty which we know to have their warrant in the real annals of crime and suffering,—but the contemplation of which true taste rejects. [. . .] if the Bells, singly or collectively, are contemplating future or frequent utterances in Fiction, let us hope that they will spare us further interiors so gloomy as the one here elaborated with such dismal minuteness.

"True taste" also rejected *The Wire*, for similar reasons.

When the article linking *The Wire* to *Wuthering Heights* appeared in the *Review*, Charlotte had not only just lost her sister, but was in the midst of work on *Shirley*, her second novel. Smith Williams, her reader at the publishing firm Smith, Elder, & Co., had asked whether she had considered writing a serial, but Charlotte seemed to lack the confidence to write a work in pieces, spread out over time.

Charlotte to William Smith Williams, December 1847:

> I think it would be premature in me to undertake a serial now; I am not yet qualified for the task: I have neither gained a sufficiently firm footing with the public, nor do I possess sufficient confidence in myself, nor can I boast those unflagging animal spirits, that even command of the faculty of composition, which, as you say and I am persuaded, most justly, is an indispensable requisite to success in serial literature. I decidedly feel that ere I change my ground, I had better make another venture in the 3 vol. novel form.

Reading these sentiments, we wonder whether Charlotte felt that H.B. Ogden possessed the "unflagging animal spirits" of which she spoke, as his serial strung out longer than most, and she obviously admired it. She met him in passing, later in life, and remarked in a letter as to his frightful whiskers, his fiery eyes—descriptions which, as any *Jane Eyre* reader can attest, she might not have deemed unattractive. Certainly any author, to continually produce so sprawling a narrative with so many intricate pieces at a regular pace, must have had a great deal of energy and vigor. While she also admired Thackeray, Charlotte reserved her highest praise of serial novelists for H.B. Ogden.

The novel she did write, *Shirley* (published under Charlotte's own pseudonym, Currer Bell) was, unbeknownst to Charlotte at this time, to share some of the reception of *Heights*. Critics condemned the first chapter especially, calling it vulgar and uninteresting. In a letter to William Smith Williams, her friend and correspondent at the firm that published her, dated November 1, 1849, Charlotte states, "Is the first chapter disgusting or vulgar? It is not; it is real."

In *Shirley*, Charlotte tried to address the "melodrama" of which her critics accused her in *Jane Eyre*, writing a novel she felt to be more realistic. As Charlotte's novels obviously attest, she was not obsessed with painting an exact picture. "You are not to suppose," she states, in a letter to her friend Ellen in the same year, "any of the characters in Shirley intended as literal portraits." She was, however, very keen on the idea of art as a means of expressing "Truth": "The first duty of an Author is—I conceive—a faithful allegiance to Truth and Nature; his second, such a conscientious study of Art as shall enable him to interpret eloquently and effectively the orders delivered by those two great deities," (Charlotte to William Smith Williams, August 14th, 1848). *The Wire* is a work littered with literal portraits, but though it is as unlike *Shirley* as *Wuthering Heights*, Charlotte no doubt admired its efforts to address "Truth."

Shirley cannot be called a "social novel" as the works of Dickens, Ogden, and Gaskell can, as it is at heart a love story, rather than one that directly addresses class tensions. The work, however, takes on some of the same concerns as novels by those three authors, and is set against the historical (for the time; the novel is set in 1811-2) backdrop of the textile industry; mill workers riot against the manufacturer, Moore, and the heroine incites him to change his ways. This is the birth of unions; naturally Charlotte would have been invested in *The Wire* as a work which exposed the conditions of lower classes.

Like Elizabeth Gaskell, Brontë argued for tenderness, feeling that human understanding could ease the way between workers and masters, industrialists and the masses. Hers was what could be called a "Christian socialism," whereas the philosophy in *The Wire* is not particularly religious and far more pragmatic. Still, both saw a hopelessness to the situation between classes.

Amanda Reese, in volume two of *The Wire*, tells Frank Sobotka, "Name names, and come clean. You help yourself, and your union." Frank answers, "Help my union? For twenty-five years we've been dyin' slow down there. Dry dock's rustin', piers standin' empty. My friends and their kids like we got the cancer. No life-line got thrown all that time, nothin' from nobody, and now you wanna help us? Help me?"

Charlotte Brontë writes the true answer to Frank in *Shirley*: "As to the sufferers, whose sole inheritance was labour, and who had lost that inheritance—who could not get work, and consequently could not get wages, and consequently could not get bread—they were left to suffer on; perhaps inevitably left."

If Ogden ever responded to "Bell's" missive, we have no record of it. We do, however, have record of his reply to the *Westminster Review*, which demonstrates his unrelenting dedication to realism and his disdain for much of the popular literature of the time:

To the editor of the <u>Westminster Review</u>,

This January your publication printed a piece of analysis regarding in the loosest of sense my serial, <u>The Wire</u>. Toward this doggerel in the guise of criticism, I would turn my pen, were the writer's cowardly name attached to his wilted, half-formed prose. Instead I suppose it attached to the public stalls of certain back alleys of this city, where he undoubtedly finds a more welcoming receptacle for his filth.

The gentleman in question (the affixment of "man" to "gentle" proving questionable in this case, due chiefly to lack of both attribution of his opinions and possibly the lack of his organs of generation, known by medical science to impart in those rarest of cases some small measure of courage) is in error in every way conceivable. He could not be more in error should he take a random selection of his lead type and throw it into the air as a child might dabble in his filth. In fact, your gentleman might find this method of composition preferable, as it is less likely to be taken as gospel by those that might peruse your publication.

That the reviewer should have difficulty understanding my writing I have no doubt—indeed, I have little doubt this would be the case with any form of communication more sophisticated than the simplest of declarative phrases, or the utterances of the animals—who, having no words, must rely upon tone and scent alone. For those with the barest modicum of intelligence, however,

The Wire is as difficult as is required for the subjects with which it deals. The institutions of man are not a birch tree, or a piece of coal, to be contained and put away by a few words of description in order that an author may spend his words upon the depiction of some great battle or the finery of a woman's dress. I could hurl a hundred thousand words into the abyss and still not have adequately conjured the frameworks which invisibly direct the lives of those born into them. Every word that I spend to coddle my reader, to please him, to lighten his heart rather than opening his eyes, is a word that is wasted.

As for my serial's supposed relation to Wuthering Heights, I should have no further comment, other than to suggest that, if Bell or any other fiction populist wishes to portray the lives of the miserable and the wretched, he would do well to focus not solely upon the twisted turns of emotion and circumstance so common among the stories of man, but also cast his eye upon the circumstances of his characters. We are all, in the end, creatures of our circumstances, and in our time, these circumstances are of man's own creation.

I am, most respectfully,
violently displeased
& dissatisfied,

H.B. Ogden

The volume set of *The Wire* was released one year after completion of *The Wire*'s initial syndication. During that year, Ogden battled the publishing company, Foxe, Warner, and Cable, who alternately wanted to abridge the text or add in further chapters or scenes which they thought may make it more palatable to a wider audience. Besides one small concession, the penning of two now-lost sketches of the history of Proposition Joe and Omar Little, Ogden resisted.

There is also some suggestion that Ogden made some tentative steps towards another serial, but no publication was forthcoming, and at this late date all that exists is rumour and implication. If Ogden did continue to write, it was without hope of publication or audience save himself; the ultimate commercial failure of *The Wire* all but guaranteed the end of his public career.

This photo, most likely of Ogden, was found with his letters and papers,
and would have been taken shortly before the end of his life.

Almost a decade after the publication of the volume set, Horatio Bucklesby Ogden died of causes not recorded. It is tempting in the face of no evidence at all to supply an ending for him suitable to the life he chose for himself, but no such neat solution presents itself; he died as most men have died through history—quietly, purposelessly, unheralded, and unremarked. Any interest in his work that had lingered during the interval between syndication and publication of the set quickly dwindled, once the work's few fans determined the volume set offered little by way of new material.

What are we to make of a man who worked so tirelessly, so zealously, for so long, in the face of such commercial indifference, who spent the last decade of his life working without anything to show for it? Is it possible that Ogden had truly reached the limits of his own endurance, that the animal passion so admired by Brontë extinguished by overwork, sickness, or simple aging, thus killing the will to battle to make his work known? Or did Ogden spend his last days fighting, secretly triumphing, in the creation of another work?

Is the finished manuscript only yet to be discovered, and will it be in that discovery that Ogden, one hundred and fifty years too late, receives the public attention he deserves?

Ogden himself would dismiss our simple optimism, our desire for a clean conclusion, as just a misguided need to see him as a hero in this story. He would remind us, in the most forceful terms, that although every man may see himself as a hero, he does so at the expense of the truth, and that to take the true measurement of a man is to see him truly for what he has done, and not what we wish him to have done.

And so the Ogden that we are left with, sans optimistic speculation, sans hopeful inference and story telling craftsmanship of any kind, is a man alone in his cramped quarters, spending the last decade of his life largely in solitude, turning his pen not to further works of fiction but to the daily matters that seem to have occupied his last years on this earth.

His final extant piece of writing, authored in the last year of his life to an unknown correspondent and presumably never sent, is startling in its ordinariness, in its remarkable lack of the incendiary tone that characterized most of his missives. His references to his health and the tremulous line of his once authoritative penmanship might suggest that a weariness and resignation had overcome him. It is also possible, however, to read a kind of peace and acceptance into what are, from our vantage point, the final words of his life.

Virginia,

It is fall again.

I don't know why I should tell you this, except that my vantage point on this season is much closer than yours, being insulated from the chill by neither young age and optimism nor by the rugged stone walls of your villa. From my window I see the shifting garb of the passers-by, see the way in which they bundle themselves and brace for the inevitable icy grip. The days grow shorter, the nights grow colder, and every face of every man below me now is wreathed in ragged cloth to hold off the season—as though they could.

As for myself, I find it more difficult to adjust my routine than I have in the past, save for a few small concessions to the cold. The other exception is, as always, my mind, as I have been even more prone to indulging those melancholies that periodically overtake me, of which I know you do not approve.

But they are what I have, nevertheless, and while they do provide me with some degree of satisfaction. It seems that, if there be no necessity of action or no object upon which to act, a man will turn his mind upon himself, much as dog, left to his own devices, will chase his own tail. In cases of extreme abandonment, dogs will even begin to chew.

It is to my estimation of myself, and others' estimation of me, I turn. (You will also know these thoughts when you are older, I have no doubt.) I have not been a great man—at this late date there is little hope of redemption. Nor have I been a good man, though I have at times considered myself so. I have not been admired, and have indeed been hated, for reasons both good and ill, reasons you know as well as me.

But the days grow shorter, the world grows colder, and though I cannot see them from my little window, somewhere there are leaves and they are falling. And even during this season of encroaching darkness I find it impossible to look back upon my life and be wholly disappointed by the labours to which I put my years. When we are young we believe solely in the reality of that which we can see, the world around us existing in relation to ourselves alone. Witness an infant's delight in the disappearance and sudden reappearance of a parent's face or a favourite toy. But as that child grows he must learn of the permanence of these things, even while he comes to grips with the seeming impermanence and inconstancy of others.

At the height of my labours, some fifteen years ago from this date, I believed as the infant believes, that to be real is to be seen, that a work unseen has indeed no reality at all, and that for the face of my audience to turn away from me would mean death to the work itself.

I was the infant; now I am the man.

From BOOK V
Excerpt CHAPTER LVII. "Took."
(February 17, 1852)

Miss Greggs, having fallen asleep in the wing-back chair by the fire, was startled to wake and find little Elijah observing her. She inquired as to whether he wanted to sleep, but he shook his head, and she sighed. He was a small enough boy that Miss Greggs might gather him in her arms, and so she did, knowing it was the duty of a mother to put a child to bed. Never once having done it before, she wondered as to the best way to do so. Hill would not be awake at this hour, and Miss Greggs was loathe to wake her, as her maid possessed a temper which had been tried that day most thoroughly in attempts to obtain a bed box in which the child might sleep. Therefore Miss Greggs carried Elijah into the kitchen herself, hoping that they might find some cold hunks of cheese from the night before or some such sustenance. Finding nothing to appeal, she carried Elijah into the morning room, though dawn was yet far away.

"Let's see," said Miss Greggs' sitting beside the window and pulling back the heavy drapes. Elijah settled upon her skirts, and they looked out the window. "Let's say goodnight to everybody. Goodnight moon. Now you say it."

"Good night moon," said Elijah obediently.

"Good night stars."

"Good night stars," said Elijah.

As if on cue, a carriage clopped by just then in the dark of the night, heralded by shouts. Miss Greggs recognized the equipage of Scotland Yard. "Good night po-po," she called.[1]

"Good night po-po."

"Good night thieves," said Miss Greggs.

"Good night thieves."

"Good night hoppers," said Miss Greggs.[2]

---

[1] **po-po**: slang for policeman, similar to "Peelers"

[2] **hoppers**: Victorian source *Urban Dictionary*, 1832-56 cites: "young, street-level miscreant"

"Good night hoppers."

"Good night hustlers," said Miss Greggs.

"Good night hustlers."

Though Elijah did not recognize the nursery rhyme, the rhythm of it gradually lulled him to sleep, for which Miss Greggs was grateful.[3] She did not, in fact, remember the rhyme herself, for though she remembered being comforted by the patterns of fairy stories, their contents had not remained set within her mind. Perhaps they were too far removed from her own experience among the dirt and ugliness of this very real world; perhaps magic rabbits and castles lay crushed somewhere under the wheel of carriages among ruts in the road, or choked by the chug of chimneys, blocking the moon half with smoke. But still did she remember the form of those children's fables, the structure of how to tell it; she remembered, "good night," and, "once upon a time." And perhaps it is these things that comfort us, not the content of our stories, but the telling of them. For Miss Greggs may speak of police and thieves, of miscreants and knaves, and still would Elijah be nodding off to sleep; perhaps there is an arrangement of the human mind which is receptive to rhythm and to rhyme, and receives information better when it is wrapped up in this framework. How would Elijah have slept, had she told him of murder, and of crime? We none of us would drift to sleep, were we to look down upon our streets and see the police and thieves, without stories told to comfort us.

"Good night to everybody," said Miss Greggs.

"Good night to everybody," said Elijah.

Miss Greggs brushed back the hair from the sweet forehead of her young charge, softly laying her lips upon his brow. "Good night to one and all."

Said Elijah, "Good night to one and all."

---

[3] **nursery rhyme**: Greggs is quoting a nursery rhyme which would have been known at the time. It is not one of the classic rhyming ditties which appeared in plays and marginalia in early centuries, but rather the result of the shift from education to entertainment in children's literature. This shift coincided with the Industrial Revolution and was probably a result of commercialism. John Newbury's *Mother Goose* collection was one of the first times many classic rhymes appeared in print, in around the 1760s. *Goodnight Moon* appeared much later, about half a century before *The Wire*, probably in the 1790s. It became very popular in the late Regency Era, and was quoted in a play called *Clockers*, which appeared ten years before *The Wire*. This scene is lifted almost directly from the play.

AFTERWORD:

Time does not turn back upon itself. The sun hurls its radiation into the surrounding void; paper decays, film unspools, the dead do not live again. But in some cases, in some small moments, comes the chance of redemption.

Initially, we could find no references to Ogden, Black, or *The Wire* in any personal correspondence, publications, or documentation of any kind dating after 1871. That changed, however, when we learned of a lost work by the filmmaker Gregory Vast.

Gregory Vast became involved in the dramatic arts at a young age. Initially lauded as a virtuoso, he became widely known in America in the early 1930s for his radio plays. These broadcasts could be startlingly realistic, at times pushing the envelope between fact and fiction in a way that alarmed the public. By the time he began making his first film, *Listen Carefully*, audiences were waiting with bated breath to see the results of his uncanny renderings of reality.

Existing telegrams between Vast and the studio suggest that an adaptation of *The Wire* was his own idea, but it's likely that any worried studio executives at Republic Pictures would have been easily persuaded due to the lurid nature of the subject matter. What they apparently weren't prepared for was the strange faithfulness of Vast's adaptation, and the lengths he was prepared to go to preserve the pacing of the original material. Obviously, the studio wasn't aware of Vast's profound respect and affection for *The Wire*. (We believe Vast to be responsible for the re-release of the novel, although naturally the bowdlerized version which resulted in 1935 would have been the opposite of his intention.)

Telegrams also suggest that Vast intended to lovingly recreate the municipal drama of *The Wire*, as well as its searing social commentary. As in *The Wire*, no social pillars were considered sacred; with *Listen Carefully*, Vast intended to criticize not only crime, but law, education, government, unions, and notably, journalism. Due to the time period in which it was written, it is sometimes difficult to identify characters in *The Wire* as representations of actual historic figures. *Listen Carefully*, however, contains more than one portrait based on powerful men of the 1930s, a fact that may have led to what happened after its release.

Shortly after completing the rough cut of *Listen Carefully*, Vast left to oversee the shooting of another film. He was only on the project for a few weeks, however, before he found out via telegram that something was wrong back in California. The studio, it seemed, was less than thrilled with the picture. When he inquired as to the source of their dissatisfaction, he at first received halting, diplomatic replies, that over the next few days dissolved into more frank language.

The studio initially received the movie coolly, but moved into full-on panic mode after screening the picture, which initially had a running time of 220 minutes. "Too boreing[sic]," one audience response card replied. "Too slow and I didn't care," said another. "Too dark, can't see the faces of the actors," read another. "I already know how depressing the world is. I don't need to see it in a film; movies are for fun," read another card. "Why should we hear about all this misery? It's artfully made, but there's no way you'll find an audience for this."

Apparently, the studio was in agreement. Although Vast's contract allowed him a hand in the initial cut, he had no such approval for the final form of the movie. Unbeknownst to him, the studio began a series of drastic cuts to the film, taking out whole reels and re-purposing elements of the original footage to fill in the gaps. Eliminating the "unnecessary" character development, long portions of dialogue and lingering, artfully composed shots, a new kind of film began to take form, one that emphasized the criminal elements and wanton violence over nuance and carefully controlled pacing.

Calling back the lead actors, Jack Wiseman, the executive in charge of Republic Pictures began filming about ten minutes of additional footage, meant to function as a moralizing, neater ending than the open-ended structure called for by Vast's adaptation of Ogden. "Inspector McNulty," as he was known in the adaptation, was given some new-hard-boiled narration, intended to cover some of the gaps left by the excised material, and to put forth McNulty as a sympathetic viewpoint character. The picture was renamed *The Death Dealers*.

When the film finally received it's limited, contractually-obligated but by no means publicised opening, it flopped. The meager audiences that happened upon the film in one of the fifty theaters in which it played had had high hopes for Vast, but found the film by turns depressing and confusing. Without the slow build of character and plot, and the careful attention to detail Vast had intended, themes of social commentary and industrial corruption fell by the wayside. Yet what was left was not an action movie, either: there was just enough realism and suggestion of current (for the time) politics that audiences found it dull and overly complex. *The Death Dealers* enjoyed limited release to no commercial success, and shortly thereafter, spent its time rotting in film canisters, and eventually a studio burn pile, all but a few feet of a single reel currently extant.

Vast did not work in Hollywood again, though he continued to attempt to make money to finance his independent film projects, all of which were also commer-

Some of the few surviving frames of *Listen Carefully*, I.E. *The Death Dealers*

cial failures. He died in 1961 of congestive heart failure, at a gallery opening for his friend and lover, collage artist Sidney Poutin.

Vast never gave any interviews about *The Death Dealers*, and for its part the studio seemed happy to be able to put the whole mess behind them. If not for the existence of the telegrams and a handful of surviving documents, the whole affair might have been forgotten.

It's hard to evaluate a film based only on hearsay and argument, and a handful of frames. What cannot be in doubt, however, is this—however deft the acting, however artfully arrayed and moodily-lit the sets, *The Wire* could never have been anything but a failure as a piece of visual media. The story is too beholden to the serial format, to the idiosyncratic rhythms of Ogden's prose to work in the crude form of the motion picture, in which the audience, rather than creating a world in conjunction with the author, has his aesthetic experience doled out to him, every moment unreeling at the same speed, the string of frames unyielding, unrelentingly timed. The moving image is too crude a form to tell the kind of stories Ogden had told, and his tale too beholden to its form. *The Wire* is not Cinderella, or Robin Hood, or the birth of Christ, a story so direct and elemental as to be impervious to manipulation and transference. It is of the written word alone. Even assuming that Vast had been able to carry out his initial plan of adapting the entirety of *The Wire* into a series of films, rather than the scant one that he had been able to complete, even given the (extremely unlikely) supposition that he would have been able to maintain even a fraction of the complexity of the book, there would still be at its heart the inherent limitations of that flickering pacifier that is the film medium. Crude, almost inherently violent and exploitative, music moronically punctuating every motion and emotion, telling us what to feel, how to react, modern visual media in all its forms eliminates nuance. And as Vast's story ably demonstrates, commercial consideration trumps all.

The argument could be made that this was true for Ogden as well, that he made his art despite the aims of his publishers, but the increased financial burden of film makes those considerations the only considerations. In Hollywood, money is what speaks. When it seemed as though *Listen Carefully* would not profit, it became *The Death Dealers*.

Truth be told, there will in all likelihood never be a modern equivalent of *The Wire*. Financial stakes are too high, audiences too impatient, and writers not considerate enough, not understanding and forgiving. If this is an indictment of ourselves as well, let it be so. We would be unwilling to give a work like *The Wire* the kind of time and attention it deserves, which is why it has faded away, instead of being elevated, held to that most exalted height as the literary triumph it truly is. If we do not open our eyes, works like *The Wire* will only continue their slow slide into obscurity.

Down in the Hole: The unWired World of H.B. Ogden

© 2012 Joy DeLyria & Sean Michael Robinson
Illustrations © 2012 Sean Michael Robinson

Published in the United States by powerHouse Books,
a division of powerHouse Cultural Entertainment, Inc.

37 Main Street,
Brooklyn, NY 11201-1021
T 212.604.9074
F 212.366.5247
downinthehole@powerhousebooks.com
www.powerhousebooks.com

First edition, 2012

Library of Congress Control Number: 2012936998
Hardcover ISBN: 978-1-57687-602-2

Printing and binding by RR Donnelley

Book design by Alex Martin and Emily Stage
Cover design by Sean Michael Robinson
Ogden letter illustrations by Carl Franzen Nelson

A complete catalog of powerHouse Books and Limited Editions is available upon request; please call, write, or visit our website.

10 9 8 7 6 5 4 3 2 1

Printed and bound in China